GUMBEAUX LOVE

GUMBEAUX LOVE

A NOVEL

Book 2 of the Gumbeaux Sistahs Series

JAX FREY

Gumbeaux Love
A Novel

Printed in the United States of America
First Printing, 2020

ISBN paperback: 978-1-7331582-1-3

Cover Illustration – Gumbeaux Sistahs Get Cookin' - Jax Frey

For Ginny, Wayne, Eric, and David—
My real Gumbeaux Sistah and Gumbreauxs

HAND ME MY PARASOL
BY MARY BETH MAGEE

A Poem inspired by the painting
"The Gumbeaux Sistahs in the French Quarter" **by Jax Frey**

"Hand me my parasol, dawlin',
and let's head to the Quarter.
I crave me some beignets and chicory coffee."

"Oh, yeah, sistah,
I'm right there with ya.
I could go for a big old café au lait myself."

"Call the girls and let's meet up.
We ain't got together since
Lafitte met up with Jackson, seems like."

"Or at least since last week, huh?"
"Yeah, you right."
"Remember the last time we was strolling
through Jackson Square
and dat bunch of tourists thought we was actors?

Guess we made a real impression,
with our hats and boas and umbrellas.
What would they think of us at Mardi Gras, huh?"

"Ha, they just don't understand how Gumbeaux Sistahs roll!"
"Or how we have fun!"
"Let's get the sistah-hood together.
I hear a muffaletta calling me,
with a cup of gumbo on the side,
and then beignets for dessert.

Good food and good friends…the secret of living rich."
"Yeah, you right, sistah. Get on the phone.
We got some living to do."

"And some loving to share."
"And some second lining to dance."
"Amen, sistah!"
© 2019 Mary Beth Magee www.LOL4.net

"Oh, I never order gumbo when I go out.
I already know that mine's the best."
Housewife, Vermillion Parish,
National Geographic 2011

"You're not gonna see many skinny Cajuns."
Chef, Houma, National Geographic 2011

PROLOGUE

"*Oh dear Lord! He's coming over!*" thought Judith, her eyes wide with panic and her feet pointing themselves towards the front door, wanting to make a run for it.

She was sitting in a bookstore and coffeehouse in Fairhope, Alabama, next door to the hotel where she was staying the night. Judith was in town to deliver some of her art to a local gift shop called *4 Bags*, and to enjoy a one-day-vacation by herself doing whatever she wanted. She had wandered around Section Street and the surrounding area, taking in the charming shops, restaurants, and beautiful flower displays on every corner. She liked to stay in Fairhope when she was delivering in that part of the coastal south. It had a charming downtown and a gorgeous, inviting beach where she had taken an early morning stroll, coffee in hand. Tomorrow, she would take that stroll one more time then hit the road back to her hometown of Covington, Louisiana.

This particular bookstore boasted not only a café, but also a large back room with lots of tables and chairs and a fully stocked bar. Small music groups often performed in the venue, which could seat about sixty music lovers, including Judith on this particular evening. She had seen a flyer on the door advertising that a band called Blue Bicycle would be playing that very evening. She finished making her delivery and visiting with Sharon, one of the pleasant owners of *4 Bags*, at four-thirty. She decided to go listen to the live music, which started at five, and enjoy a glass of wine.

Judith sat at the bar, ordered a glass of pinot noir, and watched the small venue fill up with thirsty people who were getting off of work and ready to hear some local music. The band started up and her spirits perked up a notch. They had a blue grass vibe, and the lead singer used her whispery voice and shy glances to entrance the audience. Judith almost felt she had to lean in to hear the band's pure, sweet, quiet tones filling the room.

Between songs, she looked around the room. She was curious to see what sort of crowd the band drew. It looked like the room held mostly locals, their well–worn sandals and beach–tans giving them away. It was a casual, happy–to–be–off-work group, and she could tell by the greetings and conversation between tables that many of them knew each other. At that moment, her glance stopped short at one table where she noticed a man about her age. He had drawn her eye because of his silver hair, strong shoulders, and handsome, well–tanned face. There was something contented looking about him, and she could tell that he led a happy lifestyle here in this lazy beach town. His eyes were crystal–blue, and Judith startled to realize that he was looking back at her. And smiling.

She looked away immediately, thinking, *"Oh no. Let's not. That's not why I'm here sitting at the bar alone."* She glanced back at him, and sure enough, he was still smiling at her.

"Shoot!" she thought. She had a perfect right to sit here alone and enjoy the music, but she wondered if, somehow, she was giving off signals to the kind of man who was out looking for an extra-good night. *"I'm only here for the music,"* she thought indignantly.

Several couples got up to dance in the back of the room. Judith thought about how long it had been since she had danced in public, or even how long it had been since she had been in a place like this, watching people who were out enjoying themselves. She chuckled to herself and wondered if she even remembered how to dance, though she had once been good at it. She had never been great, however, at dancing with a partner—as in holding hands and letting the other person lead. But at one point in her life she could rock and roll with the best of them. She thought back to times when she had received her share of attention on the dance floor. She had even won a dance contest at big hotel event once. She remembered making her partner look good as she danced circles around him.

She sat there reminiscing about past dances while the catchy music played, and she tapped her toes. Then, out of the corner of her eye, she registered that the handsome man was getting up from his seat and coming towards her.

"No, no, no," her mind screamed. *"Should I just chug-a-lug this wine and beat it before he gets here? I really don't want to deal with this. But, no—I don't want to leave either! I'm enjoying this music so much. OK, wait. Just calm down. I'm not going anywhere. I'll just be polite and then say 'no' and shut him down. That should send a clear message to anyone else who wants to approach. I just want to be left alone."*

He walked up, smiling, "I saw you looking at the dancers," he said with a friendly smile. "I have the feeling that you and I can show them how it's done. What do you say?" He held out his hand to her.

She frowned at him. "I really have no idea how it's done," She said bluntly, sending a more-than-clear signal.

He looked at her with a slight smirk and said, "Now why do I have a hard time believing that?," Still smiling, he leaned in closer and said softly, "C'mon - seriously, what have you got to lose? It's just a dance." His eyes twinkled at her, daring her.

She looked into those blue eyes and found an interesting invitation and a link of trust—at least about the dancing. She shocked herself completely and took his hand, thinking, *"Oh what the heck!"*

Within moments on the dance floor, Judith found herself getting into the music, adding a little twist here and a shake there as the rhythm took over. He turned out to be a great dancer. Judith got the feeling that this place was his regular stomping grounds and that he did this very thing – dancing and flirting with women – quite often, and he probably did it successfully.

They danced two songs before he led her back to her drink which was still waiting for her at the bar. To her consternation, instead of leaving her there, he ordered them both another round. She tried to refuse, but the drinks showed up anyway.

He asked her a few questions about herself and also talked to some people nearby at the bar that he knew. She actually enjoyed this part for a moment because she enjoyed meeting the locals in a new place. What she did not like was how he hovered around her possessively, sometimes lightly touching her arm and introducing her as if they were together.

He mentioned that he knew most people in town and that he could tell that she was from somewhere else. He asked where she lived, and she just told him that she was from out of town, making it clear that she was leaving in the morning so he would not get any ideas about getting cozy with her.

It had just the opposite effect, and he tried to take her hand, probably thinking he could take advantage of her one night in town. He slid his arm around her waist and said, "Come on, I'll walk you back to your hotel."

Judith decided that enough was enough.

"That's alright. I'll be fine," she said firmly, easing his arm off of her.

"But I want you to be safe," he said.

"Yes," she said pointedly, "I want to be safe too. So, no thank you."

His eyes were seeking hers, and she knew that he was going to persist in this vein. She considered making a scene. She hesitated, knowing how unpleasant that would be. Plus, she did not know if it would even work—he was so persistent. She decided to take the easy, cowardly way out. "Wait here. I need to find the ladies room."

He squeezed her hand and leaned in for a quick kiss. She recoiled abruptly. "I'll be right back," she said.

She walked away, escaped out the side entrance, and hurried back to her hotel room. She was out of practice with all of this. When she was younger, she would have shut him down in a heartbeat. Now she wasn't used to so much male attention. But she was used to being polite.

Back in her room, she changed into her pajamas, settled for a protein bar for dinner, and got into bed with the TV remote.

Before she turned on the set, she looked around the hotel room and wondered what it would be like to be with someone again romantically. She knew that she did not want that pushy man from the bar in her room, but she wondered why she never had anyone with her. A thought occurred to her for the first time in years, *"Why am I always alone?"*

CHAPTER 1

Six women sat at the back table of a cooking class, but only one of them was considering mayhem.

On the outside, Dawn Berard was her usual well put together, not-a-hair-out-of-place self, but inside she was seething. Her day out was spoiled. The daytrip to New Orleans had been her sister Trinity's idea. Trinity lived in the French Quarter and thought it would be a hoot to get the Gumbeaux Sistahs together for a cooking lesson at the New Orleans School of Cooking a few blocks from her house. The class, *Ga-Ga over Gumbo*, was taught by an old friend of Trinity's from their childhood neighborhood of Breaux Bridge, Louisiana. Rocky Breaux was now the head chef and teacher of the cooking school, and he and Trinity had once been pals in grammar school. Dawn remembered him as a scrawny kid with a loud laugh. He used to get on Dawn's nerves a bit when she was a young teen trying to get her homework done. Rocky and Trinity would listen to the radio a little too loudly and play checkers in the Robichaux family living room after school.

Now here he was, all these years later, still getting on Dawn's nerves.

The day had started well enough. Dawn drove Bea, Judith, Helen, and Lola across the Causeway bridge to New Orleans to meet Trinity for the class. They made it across the bridge, which ran twenty–four miles across Lake Ponchartrain, without incident—which was saying a lot for Dawn. She was terrified of driving over all that water, but after six months of practicing weekly trips across, at first with Lola by her side and then by herself, she was finally able to accomplish it without being tempted to close her eyes. It was a huge feat for her to conquer her fears.

At the cooking school, they found their table in the back of a class of about thirty students, all eager to learn to make gumbo, and even more eager to eat it afterwards. Rocky immediately came over to hug Trinity and to meet the other Sistahs. When his eyes lit on Dawn, he hollered, "Oh my gravy!" His smile stretched across his boyish face. "I can't believe it's you, Dawn!" Then he laughed loudly. "If it isn't the Badass of Breaux Bridge!"

Dawn was initially delighted to see the boy—now the man— that she had babysat so many times in her past, and she had been smiling at first. But when she heard her old nickname, her smile disappeared. That nickname still stung, and it was the first time in her life that she had heard Rocky use it. She never felt that she had deserved such a nickname. It had been foisted upon her and it had always made her feel cheap and tough in school.

She remembered the evening when her father first found out about the nickname. They had been sitting on the front porch of their home. A car full of teenagers roared by in the night and they yelled out "Hey Badass!" She had cringed when she saw the expression on her gentle father's face.

"Dawn, I don't think your mother would have liked that name for you," he said quietly.

"Dad, it wasn't my idea," she answered. "It's just what they call me. I'm doing the best I can to make them stop." Her face was red with the shame of disappointing him.

Her father looked at her with kind eyes. "You always do your best, honey," he said. "Don't worry, it will change, and it will get better too."

"Hope you're right," she said with a quiet, deep sadness.

Dawn and Trinity's mother had died when they were very young. Their father was disabled, but he still worked as a custodian at Dawn's school. Dawn was left to play mother to Trinity and their young brothers. Rocky Breaux, who lived up the street from Dawn and Trinity, was often at their house to play after school and on weekends. She remembered Rocky's mother being extremely kind to them when Dawn's mother passed, going out of her way to help with the funeral.

One thing she did not remember from the old days, or maybe she was only vaguely aware of it back then, was the fact that Rocky was obviously gay. He was still much shorter than Dawn—most people were—and he had kept his wiry countenance, high voltage energy, and vivacity. His infectious smile was still there, and he still that crazy laugh. He had apparently maintained his wise-acre, smart-aleckiness as well. He was a terrible tease back then. Now he was teasing her again in class, "Dawn, it's good you came. Someone can finally teach you to make something besides mac and cheese!"

Dawn, who prided herself greatly on her abilities in the kitchen, felt a hot red anger creep up to her ears. Two sentences out of Rocky's mouth was enough to bring back the painful days of her youth. Now she was downright annoyed. Rocky had been around during some of the poorest years of their lives. There were many nights when boxed mac and cheese was the family dinner because their Dad worked long hours for little pay, and there was not much money for food. Plus, Dawn had had little time between school and homework to take care of the kids and do the cooking and housework. Her mother had taught her to cook some things before she passed, including some truly awesome things like her gumbo. Dawn had been a good cook then and was an excellent cook now, but it had been a challenge to do everyday meals at the age of fifteen. Unfortunately, after his own mother died, Rocky was often at their table, and macaroni was what they usually had to eat.

Rocky took his place in the front of the cooking class. His stove had mirrors placed just so to allow the students to watch his cooking instructions step by step. The sistahs had settled in to pay attention when suddenly Judith chose that moment to blurt out of nowhere, "A man almost kissed me Friday night!"

A couple of the sistahs had reached for their iced tea right before she spoke and almost choked on the cold liquid. "What?" yelped Dawn. "You couldn't mention this on the drive over?"

"I know!" said Judith. "I should have said something, but I can't sit here for the next hour without mentioning it now." She was almost as surprised as they were at the words that had come flying out of her mouth. She had meant to wait and tell them after class when there was time. "I wasn't going to say anything, and then it just came out. I can't help it. I keep thinking about it!"

"I can't believe you held that in as long as you did!" said Trinity.

"Tell us everything—and I mean now!" said Lola excitedly.

Dawn was simply bamboozled and folded her arms firmly. "Judith Lafferty, just start talking," she said.

At the front of the room Rocky was just beginning to sauté the onions, bell pepper, and celery for the gumbo, when he stopped short and looked Dawn's way. He grinned and said in a sing-song voice, "Looks like someone thinks they can teach this class. Whoops, I forgot, Dawn. You can't cook!"

Titters from the rest of the class were heard around the room and Dawn felt her blood boil.

Trinity saw the look on her sister's face and started to say, "Dawn, don't get all crazy."

But it was too late. Boiling-mad now, Dawn stood up and put both hands on her broad hips, "Rocky Breaux, how dare you! The day you can teach me anything about cooking is the day pigs fly. And pigs never fly, in case you didn't learn that in cooking school." She looked the sistahs. "Y'all can stay here and listen to this little twerp, but I'm done." She turned to the class and announced loudly, "I used to babysit this guy back home in Breaux Bridge. My sister used to try to teach him to dance in our living room, and let me tell you—that was another thing he could never learn to do. He looked like a gawky monkey stomping around our living room. So, I wouldn't vouch for his cooking either, but you folks are welcome to take your chances." She turned back to Trinity. "I'll be around the block at Tableau's having a French 75. Come find me when you're done."

She picked up her purse and started making her way across the room. "You have some nerve, Rocky. We took you into our family back then. We tried to teach you to dance and while that didn't work,

I can surely still teach you a thing or two about cooking. And as for gumbo, I can cook it with my eyes closed!"

"Oh my gravy! And I'm sure it would taste as if you did too, honey" said Rocky, smirking.

"Monkey dancer!" shouted Dawn and opened the door. Before walking out, she turned back towards the sistahs, "And Judith Lafferty, don't you say one more word about that kiss till you come find me!"

"Will I ever learn to keep my big mouth shut?"
- Judith

CHAPTER 2

awn walked around Jackson Square trying to blow off <u>some</u> steam. "*That Rocky has some nerve,*" she fumed. She rolled quickly down the cobbled streets, passing the horse-drawn carriages and the outdoor artists selling brightly painted canvases hanging on the iron fence surrounding the square. Crossing Decatur Street, she walked up to the river-front and looked back at St. Louis Cathedral at the edge of the square. Dawn had always considered it one of the most beautiful city-scenes in the world. The scores of visitors to the city taking photos right in that very spot, no doubt, would have agreed with her.

She headed over to Tableau restaurant, ordered a cocktail, and chose a table by the window so she could people-watch. By the time the girls got out of class and joined her, she was on her second French 75 and in a much better mood. It did not last long.

Trinity walked in saying, "You sure got Rocky all wound up! Why didn't you just let it go?" She plopped into the closest chair. "After you left, he vented for at least five minutes about how some people can't hold their liquor! I knew he was kidding—you know Rocky—but it was embarrassing. And then he started in again on how you couldn't cook back in Breaux Bridge, and that it was a good thing you left today because you couldn't be trusted around his kitchen."

"What?" bellowed Dawn, her eyes widening and her mouth dropping open. "I should sue that little twerp for slander! Are you kidding me?"

"I'm afraid she's not, dear," said Bea. "It was kind of hard to hold our tongues."

"Or it would have been if it hadn't been so funny. Rocky is hilarious," said Lola, grinning.

"How nice," said Dawn, disgustedly. Then she looked at Trinity, "I hope that, as my little sister, at least you had my back."

Trinity was quiet, and the other women looked at the floor and the ceiling—everywhere except at Dawn.

"Trinity, you did back me up, right? You didn't let him get away with that, did you?"

"I did—a little," said Trinity hesitantly. "But Dawn, you have to realize that Rocky has no idea what a great cook you are. He only remembers you cooking when you were a teenager and hadn't learned everything you know now. And you didn't have time to cook back then anyway. Honestly, you have to admit, all that mac and cheese? We had some pretty awful meals back then. We ate them anyway because it was all we had, but they were pretty sad at times. Rocky and I used to laugh about it growing up. That's all he knows about your cooking. We even used to tease you about it back then, remember? Rocky was just carrying on like we used to. I understood that. To tell you the truth, I was really surprised when you blew up at him."

"Just so we're clear, I will blow up each and every time somebody insinuates that I don't know my way around a kitchen. It's my thing, and you know it."

"Yes, I do," mumbled Trinity. "And I feel bad about it now. Sorry, Dawn."

"And what a little jerk he is! He actually said that I can't hold my liquor in front of all those people? That is so humiliating! Incidentally, which one of you is driving home?" She took another sip of her champagne cocktail and went on, "Plus he used that nickname that I hated—I still hate it. He knows that!"

Helen, ever the diplomat and hiding a smile, changed the subject. "It's too bad you left. Judith got up and told the whole class about the guy who tried to kiss her."

At this, Dawn leaped to her feet, "No! I missed it? Judith, how could you?"

Judith grinned. "Helen's just yanking your chain. Do you really think I'd tell a roomful of people about my love life?"

"No, come to think of it, I don't," conceded Dawn. Then she added with a sly grin, "Love life, huh?"

"Whatever you want to call it. I mean, good Lord, I don't even talk about it to y'all—much less a cooking class!"

"That's true," said Bea. "But you know you can talk about anything with us, dear. I think we've shown you that by now."

"But it's nothing, really," said Judith. She told them all about her delivery day in Fairhope and about the man at the live-music event dancing with her, trying to kiss her, and doing his best to walk her back to her hotel.

"You should have kissed him," said Lola, nodding.

"Well, we all know you would say that," said Dawn, grinning. "We're all aware of your reputation—prior to Bud, that is."

"What? I'm just saying it might have been fun for Judith—a little adventure," said Lola defensively.

"Yes, we all know about your adventures, Lola," laughed Dawn.

"Dears, we all know Lola means nothing but the best for Judith," said Bea reassuringly.

"You know, she may have a point," said Judith. "I can't stop thinking about it. It might have been fun. I'm not sure why I didn't kiss him." She was quiet for a moment then went on, "I know I've never said anything like this to any of you because, most of the time, I'm just fine with the way my life is. In fact, I love it. But every once in a while, I do get lonely."

You could have heard a pin drop at that table, and Judith realized immediately that she should have kept her big, fat mouth shut.

Bea drove everyone home across the lake after dropping Trinity off at her French-Quarter apartment. The Sistahs talked about the cooking class, Rocky's humor, Dawn's outburst, Tableau's French 75's, the smoothness of the lake as they crossed the Causeway, and many other things that had happened during their day out.

They dropped Judith off first. The minute she was out of the car, Dawn turned to the Sistahs and said, "OK, what are we going to do about her?"

CHAPTER 3

That night, Dawn settled onto her comfy, white couch with a glass of Pinot Noir and her laptop. Dan, her husband, was out of town at an accounting conference in Atlanta, so she had the quiet house to herself. The day's events weighed heavily on her mind, and she knew that sleep was going to be hard to come by. So, she resorted to the one activity she knew for certain could take her mind off of things and relax her enough to go back to bed. The wine didn't hurt either.

The activity that helped Dawn relax was of the secret, late-night sort. She did not take part in it often, but when she did, it was oddly satisfying. It brought a mischievous glint to her eye, her heart quickened, and a smile played about her lips. She found it stress-relieving and it made her feel like she was getting away with something, all at the same time, which she was. That was best part.

She signed into Facebook and grinned in anticipation. A few days ago, she had looked up Rocky Breaux and friended him since she knew she would be seeing him shortly at the cooking class.

Thinking of the class again made her blood boil. *"That little twerp!"* she seethed. Why would he try to humiliate her in public like that? And how dare he call her that hated nickname! She questioned whether she would be able to sleep for the next week—much less that night.

The truth was that what Rocky said had really hurt. Dawn had been like a second mother to him when they were young. He was at the Robichaux house more than he had been at his own, and he and Trinity had been inseparable for many years. Dawn had had to shoo him out the door in the evening after he had dinner with her family, or else he might never have left. And yes, in some ways he was right about her cooking. They did have simple, cheap meals most nights. She was only a young teenager herself back then—a teenager with a heavy responsibility caring for younger siblings after their mom had died. She had thrown together meals like scrambled eggs, frozen pizza from the discount grocery, lima bean sandwiches, and the famous boxed mac and cheese. She had made large pots of red beans, which they ate with rice all week. It came down to whatever she could scrape together on a slight budget and limited time. Her brothers and sister, and even her father, never protested. It was just the way it was.

So, it was a shock to hear Rocky complaining to her forty years later, after her family had accepted him into the house so often and fed him when they could barely feed themselves. He never wanted to go home. His mom was gone. Dawn had not made a big deal of his being around their house so much because she knew what it was like to lose a mother. Besides, he had given Trinity someone to talk to, which was more than Dawn had ever had.

Dawn had her share of boyfriends back then, but did not feel very comfortable sharing everything she was going through with them. She could have used a friend, but she always had a great deal of difficulty making them. The kids at school liked to mock her, her clothes, and the family's house, mostly because of their obvious poverty. Dawn had learned to toughen up because of the bullying that they had suffered. Eventually, those that bullied her family learned that it came with a price.

After that, the bullies gave her grief about was her reputation. She became the *Badass of Breaux Bridge*. Initially it was done mockingly, not seriously. She was not a true, serious badass when it first started. She grew into it.

And to hear Rocky Breaux, of all people, refer to her with that name was not only shocking, it was sickening. He knew better— no question. He had been there and had seen the damage and pain it had inflicted on Dawn and how it had hurt her father so. How dare he? The idea enraged her all over again. She shook her head and swore under her breath. Then she drew her attention back to the laptop and thought grimly, *"Oh yes, this will be fun. You've got it coming, Rocky Racoon."*

Some time ago, Dawn had discovered that it was enormously satisfying to vent on Facebook. She did not do it the way so many other people did—ranting about their politics and railing against humanity—which only served to spread more hate in the world. No, she went about it secretly. There was an element of risk to it, and that was what made it so fulfilling.

If she was angry or upset with someone for whatever reason, she would fire up her laptop very late at night and type scathing posts about them. She would even tag the person if they were Facebook friends. She would pour all of the built-up venom into her words and gleefully lay it on thick. When she got it all out of her system, she would stop and take a sip of whatever alcohol accompanied the night's rant. After she read her posts over several times until she was satisfied, she would then delete both the tag and the post. It was like throwing her fierce anger out into the wind, then sucking it all back in with a kind of emotional vacuum cleaner. It served to weaken the anger and allowed her to move past some issues she dealt with on a day-to-day basis.

Tonight, she stretched out her fingers in anticipation and began to type.

"Hey Monkey Boy, it was so good to see you today. It reminded me of the mealy-mouthed little leach you were as a kid, always mooching off of my family. And now you fancy yourself a big-time chef. Oh, please! The idea of you teaching people to cook is laughable—especially when it comes to gumbo. Let me tell you, if you ever ate my gumbo, you'd run back to Breaux Bridge with your monkey tail between your legs. In fact, I challenge you to a gumbo cook-off. But, forget it. You wouldn't dare show your face at a competition because you know what a truly excellent ass-whupping you would receive. And it would be my pleasure to administer it!"

She read it over, grinned, and then sat back in her couch, deeply rewarded. She chuckled to herself over her momentary revenge and took several sips of wine as a feeling of well-being settled over her.

Dawn opened her eyes and saw daylight streaming into the high den windows. *"Is it morning already?"* she thought. She realized that she had never slept all night on the couch before, but then Dan was not there to call her upstairs to bed. She glanced at a clock and saw that it was late, almost nine o'clock. The world was well and truly awake and starting the day without her.

She started to get up and head for the kitchen and coffee, when her eyes flew wide open. Her computer was still open. A feeling of pure dread covered her from head to toe, and she whispered, "Oh no, no, no, please no! Please let me have deleted that post before I fell asleep."

Her eyes searched the screen and found it still on her Facebook page with fifty-two likes underneath, and a comment from one Rocky Breaux that simply read, "Challenge accepted."

CHAPTER 4

Judith sat in her kitchen sipping her orange juice and gazing out of the aged, wavy glass in the windows of her hundred-year-old cottage. Her house felt cozy and solid against the wind picking up outside. The great oak tree out back stood fast against the breeze with its enormous limbs spanning her yard and encroaching on a couple of her neighbors' as well.

She felt comforted by the tree's presence. "*Why do people often feel uplifted by being near large trees, especially the older ones?*" she wondered. She thought that the comfort they offered had to be part science and part magic, no matter what people said.

Part of her thoughts this morning was on the sistahs' trip to the cooking school. She felt bad that Dawn had an altercation with Rocky, but her mind was distracted by something else as well. She was remembering the comment that she had made to the sistahs about how sometimes she felt lonely. She truly wished she had not said anything now. She was not even sure why she had. It had just blurted out of her mouth somehow – with a force all its own. And while it was true sometimes that she did get lonely, it was mostly not. Judith was alone, but almost never lonely.

She had been married more than her fair share and had had more boyfriends than she could remember. But it had been a while. Truth be told, it had been quite a long time since she had even kissed a man. Something had clicked off in her head and in her heart a while back, and she felt that she had had enough of relationships for a spell. She had wanted to concentrate on her career.

Her old job as manager of the Covington Art Museum had taken most of her time, and the years had flown by. Then, when she had lost her job a year ago, she and Dawn had opened the Gumbeaux Sistahs Gallery in downtown Covington. Her time and attention had gladly turned to creating art, running the gallery, and enjoying her new friends.

They called themselves the Gumbeaux Sistahs because of their closeness to each other and because of their love for good gumbo. They felt like sisters even though they were not related to each other by blood, except for Trinity and Dawn. They supported and loved each other, and they sometimes squabbled like sisters too, especially when it came to whose mother had the best gumbo recipe. That question would probably never be resolved because they were each so deeply convinced of the superiority of their own family recipe. And they were all correct in their own way. There was not a bad gumbo in the bunch. But that really was not a true issue that needed resolving for this group. It was their friendship that was important. The squabbling was just for fun.

With all the focus on her old job and then the new business venture, Judith realized that she had gone without male company for a long time. Not only that, but she seemed to be becoming more and more invisible. And not just invisible to the radar of men, but to everyone—men and women, young and old. Actually, it was a relief some of the time. Invisibility meant that she did not have to please anyone but herself. She dressed for herself and not to please anyone else. She ate the food she craved and enjoyed doing the activities that she wanted to do. In essence, she became more completely and authentically herself. True, she had taken it a bit too far lately and had become too solitary. But all that changed last year when the sistahs had "adopted" her. Actually, it was more like "kidnapped" her and made her one of their own. Life was very good now. But once in a while, she would feel the old twinge kick up and would think to herself, *"I wonder what it would be like to fall in love one more time."*

Bits and pieces of her relationships and marriages floated by in her mind while she sipped at her fresh-squeezed juice.

Forty years ago, she had married her college sweetheart, Earl. He was quite a wonderful man, and she had loved him very much, but she had realized before long that she had married too young. The world was a bigger place than she had imagined at first, and if she wanted to see it—and she did—she would have to go it alone.

So, they had split up and she had traveled and explored the world as much as she could. As travel often does to a person, she expanded her mind and heart. So when she met her next husband-to-be, Charles, she thought she might be wiser and ready for a family. Charles was a fascinating man—intelligent, charming, and interesting. They had children together before Judith could blink twice, four of them in all – three girls and one boy. But however interesting this husband was, he was unfortunately not a very good father. Judith's children became her main concern, and she found herself protecting them from him. He was not physically abusive, but he was narcissistic and seemingly unconcerned with their lives.

He came home from work on the weekdays, dropped into his recliner in front of the TV where he ate his dinner, and did not speak to anyone. If the children tried to talk to him, he simply ignored them. On weekends, he would disappear by himself leaving Judith and the children behind. It got to where Judith began to think of him as not a part of the family at all. Needless to say, the marriage was falling apart.

He was the children's father and would always be connected to them, but she thought he could cause them less pain if he did it from somewhere else. She remembered the day she had decided that enough was enough. The night before, Charles had stayed out until after midnight, then came home a little tipsy and disheveled. Judith had been sleeping but woke up when she heard him come in noisily through the side door. She got up and asked him if he was OK and where he had been. He barely answered her, made his way to the bathroom, dropped his dirty clothes on the bedroom floor, and crawled into bed. He was snoring inside of a minute. Judith got back in bed too but could not sleep. All of her senses were on red alert and she knew what she knew. At four-thirty, she gave up on sleep and got up, stumbling in the dark over his laundry. Picking up his shirt and socks, intending to bring them to the hamper, she got a premonition, not the first of the night. She reached inside his shirt pocket and brought out a piece of paper that read "Lila." Next to the name was phone number. Judith just knew. She did not even bother to confirm it. That was plenty enough. She took herself into the kitchen, made some strong coffee, and thought about her options. At six-thirty, she was unable to wait any longer. She went into their room, shook him by the shoulder, and explained to him quite matter-of-factly, "Wake up, Charles. It's moving day." She had his clothes packed in an hour and requested that he spend the night in a hotel. He did, and once he was out of the house, Judith never let him back in. She ended up with full custody of her four children without much of a protest on his part. He knew better.

Her next marriage was not a traditional one, although it may as well have been. She and Wes had been a couple for over ten years and ended up moving in together for the last two. They had a strange connection. They were wired together somehow. If she thought of him, he would sense it and call her on the phone in the next few minutes. Judith had a passion for the man—could not get enough of him. Until she did. She had never felt like she was completely on solid ground with him. It was as if, after ten years, he was still trying to make up his mind whether he loved her or not, even though he said he did. She was never sure whether he wanted to stay with her or leave. It broke her heart, but she made the decision for him one day.

She took a weekend trip to another city, rented an apartment, went home, quit her job, rented a moving van, and that same week she left him standing in his driveway watching her and her kids drive away. She had tears in her eyes, but she shoved a CD in the car player and listened to Jo Dee Messina sing about never looking back and drove forward to a new life.

There was a clear pattern in her life of leaving—even when it hurt like hell. She had accepted the notion that she was not the marrying type. Also, she recognized that she needed to be by herself in order to become her best self. Some people can do this while still married, Judith did not know how. But just because she was not the marrying type, that did not mean she was not the loving type.

Eventually, she ended up back in her hometown of New Orleans for a time. Then she found a house she loved across the lake in the beautiful, little city of Covington. She still heard from Wes once in a while, and if she thought of him, sure enough, he would still call that same day. In order to squelch those calls, she had learned after a while to keep those thoughts out of her head. She missed him, but it was not worth the pain to talk to him.

With all the discarded marriages, she often thought that if her life was a movie and there were awards for the category of Best Departures by a Leading Lady, she would have a shelf full of Oscars and People's Choice awards.

Since that last time, there had been mild flirtations and short-lived dating spurts now and then, but she could never find the inclination, or the heart, to go there again.

But still—once in a while . . .

"There are many kinds of love in this world, and it's a great honor in this life to feast on any of them."

- Judith

CHAPTER 5

Judith rinsed her juice glass in the kitchen sink just as the doorbell rang.

"Who in the world at this hour?" she thought, shaking her head and glancing at the clock on the wall. *"It's not even eight o'clock."*

She walked to the front door and started to open it, but before she could swing it open all the way, a hand clutching a paper coffee cup shoved its way inside, barely missing her face.

"What?" she yelped. Then she laughed. "Oh no, are you kidding me?" She opened the door to five Gumbeaux Sistahs, including Bea, Helen, Dawn, Lola, and Trinity who stood on her front stoop holding coffee. It was especially a surprise to see Trinity there since she lived across the lake and had a long way to come. But the most unexpected thing of all was Dawn, who stood there looking embarrassed as all get-out, wearing a big, red Cupid costume.

"Not again!" said Judith, rolling her eyes and remembering that this was exactly the way that the sistahs had originally kidnapped her and become her best friends in the world.

Dawn grimaced and said, "I don't know why I'm always the one who has to wear a stupid costume."

"Who is it that's always starting the trouble around here?" Lola pointed out, raising her eyebrows meaningfully at Dawn, who sighed in response. "It's not always me," Dawn mumbled.

"Are you here to kidnap me again?" asked Judith, laughing.

"No, dear. Well…OK, yes," said Bea, chuckling. "But mostly we're here to help you out again—in our own inimitable fashion, of course." Her merry blue eyes twinkled at Judith.

"Help me? Help me do what? You've already changed my life for the better. Seriously! And, Trinity, I'm really surprised to see you here. When did you come in from New Orleans? You didn't come all the way over to get dragged into this, did you?"

"I spent the night at Dawn's last night. I felt that I was needed for this assignment,"

"Assignment?" asked Judith, now truly puzzled.

"We'll tell you all about it, but first, let's go. Bitsy's waiting for us at the Gumbeaux Sistahs Gallery so she can lend a hand too."

Judith shrugged, laughing, and said, "OK, why not?" Sometimes it was easier not to argue with this group. She would find out sooner or later what this was all about.

They piled into Dawn's SUV, and two minutes later they were greeted by Bitsy at the gallery with freshly made coffee.

"Welcome to another kidnapping, Bits!" said Judith.

"Glad to be here," laughed Bitsy. "And let me say that the gallery looks great. I love these two new pieces you painted, Judith."

"Thanks," said Judith. Then she grinned, "And yes, I'm glad you could make it to yet another felony performed in broad daylight by the Gumbeaux Sistahs. Did it ever occur to y'all that if you had just asked me to show up at the gallery at a certain time, that I'd be here?"

"Yes, it did," laughed Bea. "But this is so much more our style, dear."

And Judith had to agree.

Bitsy glanced at her watch. "I can only stay a few minutes. I didn't want to miss anything, but I've got to get to work." Bitsy worked at Covington Art Museum where Judith had been employed for ten years. They had worked together for most of that time. "The boss has been riding me like crazy lately! It's been kind of miserable. I don't know what gotten into her. You haven't given her any more reasons to hate any of you, have you?" She smiled mischievously.

Lillian Deslattes, the Chairwoman of the museum board, had proven in the past to be a real challenge to the Gumbeaux Sistahs—and they to her. Her crimes against the Sistahs had included getting

Judith fired and accusing her of sleeping with Lillian's husband. Then when Dawn and Judith opened the gallery, she had tried to sabotage their opening night. But none of the Sistahs could think of anything that could have riled up the beast lately.

They all knew that hiring Bitsy, who was a techno-genius, to be the Covington Museum's Director was one of Lillian's better ideas. Lillian was lucky to have her. So, it was a surprise to hear that she was working Bitsy so hard and stressing her out.

"Thanks for firing up the coffeepot, Bits," said Dawn.

"Not a problem, but let's get to it."

"OK, she's right," said Lola. "I've got a women's rights rally in two hours and then accounts to tend to this afternoon." Lola had the heart of an activist, a law degree she seldom used except for activism work, and her name on the door as owner of the Fleur de Lis Nursery, a plant care and landscaping business. She developed beautiful outdoor designs and took care of corporate plant installations for companies such as the Southern Hotel. She also was the creator of the Living Art Sculpture at the Gumbeaux Sistahs Gallery which attracted a great deal of attention from customers. The installation included wire sculptures covered in living, green vines to resemble humans with flattering lighting and music that gave it a contemplative effect. Lola's piece and Judith's art helped put the gallery on the map very quickly, and it was a success from its opening night. A similar piece by Lola had been formerly installed in the Covington Art Museum but was no longer there, which was another source of contention with Lillian Deslattes.

Bea got right down to business. "Judith. OK, dear. Here's what we were thinking . . ."

"And this is why Dawn is dressed like a fool . . ." cut in Lola, grinning widely.

Dawn took a bow. Judith said, "Well, yes, I wondered about that, but you know—it *is* Dawn. I've come to expect anything."

"So," continued Bea, "You mentioned the other day when we were in New Orleans that there were times when you felt lonely."

"Oh, that . . ." started Judith.

Dawn interrupted with a shout, "We're gonna get you a man!"

Judith's eyes grew wide. "You're gonna what?" She felt a rising panic. It was not an unreasonable response to this group.

"Relax, Judith. And Dawn—just tone it down, OK? You're scaring our girl," said Helen. She turned back to Judith. "We just thought we could help you explore the subject, that's all."

"Like how?" asked Judith.

"Well, OK, for starters, tell me this," said Trinity. "What's the first thing you notice about a man when he approaches you?"

"The audacity!" said Judith loudly, then grinned. Lola and Dawn snorted with laughter.

Trinity rolled her eyes. "OK, other than that. What first goes through your mind?"

Judith thought about the man she had danced with in Fairhope. She remembered her initial reaction when she saw him crossing the room towards her.

"I don't know. I guess my first reaction to that sort of thing is one of distrust. I wonder what the man wants from me."

Trinity nodded. "Yeah, I can see that. Lots of people feel that way. Sometimes I even feel that way myself."

"You?" asked Dawn. "I'm surprised to hear you say that, Trinity. Your usual reaction to a stranger is to invite them over for dinner!"

"Well, I guess it is," chuckled Trinity. "But still, you can understand where she is coming from. The problem, Judith, is that that attitude is not doing you any good."

"Maybe we could help," said Helen. "I know! We could do a group meditation on opening our hearts."

"Yes, we could and probably will," said Dawn. "But I think she needs more than that. I think she needs to get into action."

"Hold up, ladies," said Judith, throwing up her hands. "I really don't need or want any help with this. If a man is supposed to show up, it will happen all by itself. I don't want to become one of those women who can only think and talk about one thing—men! I know a couple of women like that. I might not see these women for a year, then I'll run into them, and the first thing they need to tell me is their man situation. It's like they feel incomplete and spend all their time—and I mean ALL their time—in search of a guy. Then they end up with some horrible guy for company. When I see that happening, I can't help but think 'Oh thank God I'm not in that mind frame or situation.'"

"Well, sure," said Lola. "We all know women who are men-blind. I've had a touch of it myself in my past life." She laughed ruefully.

"A touch?" snorted Dawn. "Ha! With all the men you've known, it has to be more than just a touch!"

Lola ignored her. "As I was saying," she threw a derisive look at her friend in the Cupid suit. "We all have known women whose happiness is dependent on the men in their lives. It's an unhappy place to be, that's for sure. But there's nothing wrong with stretching your heart a little for the possibility of love. It might be good to take a period of time to say yes to the exploration of it. We all know you're fine and happy on your own, Judith. You're a strong woman with great kids and a pretty darned good life."

"Not to mention your amazing friends and truly fabulous business partner," laughed Dawn.

"And because you're strong, you can handle an exercise in exploring relationships. We wouldn't suggest it if it weren't true. And I mean, really, what have you got to lose?"

"There some truth there," said Judith. She had never thought of it that way before.

"We're going to make it better!" said Dawn.

"Aw, you just want to meddle," said Lola teasingly. "But the rest of us want to help."

"I'm not meddling—I'm helping. I just do it in a very personal, offensive way." said Dawn, grinning.

"What do you think, dear? Are you up for a little heart-stretching?"

Judith thought for a moment, looking around at her friends. She shrugged. "Well, I guess I really don't have anything to lose. But someone has to keep Dawn from going crazy about this, agreed?"

Lola and Trinity both spoke up, "Oh, we'll watch her."

Trinity added, "Yeah, we know how she is."

"Just how am I?" demanded Dawn.

Trinity answered by simply rolling her eyes.

"Yeah, OK. You're probably right," shrugged Dawn.

"But wait, Trinity, you didn't come all the way across the lake just for this, did you?" asked Judith incredulously.

"Of course not," answered Trinity. "I came for your makeup!"

"I'm not meddling—I'm helping. I just do it in a very personal, offensive way."

– Dawn

CHAPTER 6

"**W**hat makeup?" asked Judith, genuinely puzzled and not a little on alert.

"Your makeup, silly," said Trinity, plopping a large cosmetic case on the counter and rummaging around in it. "For the photos."

Judith looked from face to face for a clue, "Photos?"

"Yes the photos that Bitsy needs, of course," stated Trinity briskly, indicating Bitsy who sat with her laptop open on the other side of the room. Trinity pulled out numerous brushes, powders, lipsticks, primer, and foundation.

"I don't understand why Bitsy would need my photo—and I already have makeup on," said Judith with a frown.

"What you have on now is a suggestion of makeup," said Trinity matter-of-factly. "What's on that face right now is a hint of the real thing. If you're going to look your best and take a good picture, you need the real thing. And I happen to be good at it."

"She is," nodded Dawn. "She always did her friends' makeup in college, even their wedding makeup. In fact, I can remember her practicing a bit on Rocky as a joke back in middle school." She looked thoughtful and said aloud, "Hmmmm, now why didn't I see that back then?" She shook her head, "Oh well."

Trinity went on, "You've been to my house and already know that I have my own costume room. That's where Dawn's cupid costume came from, by the way. I once wore it on a Krewe of Muses Mardi Gras float. I'm glad to get some more use out of it. That room of mine is chock-full of costumes, makeup, wigs—you name it. I embrace the theatrical. It's only natural that I'd love makeup too. Now, sit over here, and let me work my magic on you." She pointed to a nearby chair, and Judith found herself plunked into it.

Helen nodded at her encouragingly, "Why not try it? That's what I always say."

"Well, I'll admit I'm curious to see what you'll do, Trinity, but why would Bitsy need pictures of me all tarted up?"

Bitsy swung her laptop around and showed her what she was working on. Several windows were open on the screen, and Judith could just make out EHarmony, Match, and something called Zoosk.

Judith jumped to her feet, "Oh dear Lord! I should have known!"

"Look, Judith, I've got you all set up already with accounts, passwords, and some basic details. I just need a photo and then you need to add a few personal statements. Read what I wrote."

Judith's eyes skimmed the page along with the other sistahs. Then she lifted her head and said disbelievingly, "Good Lord, Bitsy, you made me sound almost cool."

"I call it as I see it," smiled Bitsy. "Give me your phone, and I'll set you up with apps so you can check the sites."

"Why does this seem like a really terrible idea?" Judith asked the room.

"We have to do this right, Judith. And by that, I mean we do it big, or we go home," said Dawn, busily trying scarves and necklaces around Judith's neck for the photo.

"I'd just as soon go home," said Judith hopefully.

Lola had been standing to one side for a moment, lost in thought and watching her friends. She said slowly and mysteriously, "You do always go big, don't you, Dawn? But things don't always have to be a big deal, do they? I mean, sometimes it's fine to do things on a small, tasteful scale, don't you think?"

"What are you talking about, Lola? C'mon, we've got to go all in on this for Judith!" answered Dawn.

Lola looked at Judith and smiled, "Sorry. I've got things on my mind. Dawn's right in any case and really how often do we get to say that?" She chuckled. "You know, this may seem like a bad idea now, but anything worth doing can start out that way, right?" said Lola. "It's what you call taking a risk." She pushed Judith back down onto the chair.

"So you'll try it, dear? I would if I were you. If it doesn't work, then you just stop. Pretty simple, really," said Bea.

"Yeah, easy-peasy," said Bitsy. "Just give it a shot. If you really don't like it, you can just delete the apps and unsubscribe from the sites."

"I think it sounds like fun," said Dawn. "Too bad I'm a happily married woman. I could see how this might be a hoot!"

"Never mind her, Judith. Just try it for a little while, OK?" asked Lola, shaking her head at Dawn.

"OK, let's try it. As you say, I can always walk away."

"Atta girl!" said Bea.

Trinity began chattily applying makeup to Judith's face, "I'm so glad I have my husband, Harry. He's such a doll. My first marriage just didn't work out, and I had to divorce him. That man thought he was God, but I'm Catholic and I know better!"

Dawn laughed, patted her sister's back. "To tell the truth, I would not like to start dating right now. I've gained so much weight and my rear end is so big that it feels as if someone is following me around—very closely." She looked at Lola. "And not one comment about that from you!"

"I don't actually have to say anything more after that. You do all your own insulting these days," laughed Lola.

Judith grinned at her friends, suddenly remembering something. "You know, several years ago I joined a new singles group that was forming in Mandeville. I thought at the time, 'What have I got to lose?' But when I went to the first meeting, it was all women."

Dawn grunted, "That can't be good if you're looking to meet a man."

"Nope. Not at all. It made me realize that what they say is probably true—there's a lot more single women out there looking than there are men."

"It's doesn't matter though, all you need is one, right?" Lola asked Judith.

Judith continued, "Actually, they turned out to be quite a nice group of women, and I thought that at least I could make some good friends there. But then a couple of men showed up."

"OK good. So, things were looking up!" encouraged Dawn.

"You might think so, but those men were awful. I guess because they were the only men in a big group of women, they thought they were God's gift to the world. So arrogant. It was too much. And then the women, naturally, became very competitive over the only two men in sight. It wasn't fun anymore."

"Yuck," said Helen.

"Yeah. Honestly, I don't have a lot of patience for male arrogance—well, any arrogance, really."

"I think some of it might be in their DNA," said Bitsy. "But men are not all bad. It comes in varying degrees. Some are wonderful."

"You're right, and I do know quite a few men who seem to be lovely. They're all married, of course. Maybe they're lovely because they're married, what do you think?"

"Different strokes, dear," said Bea. "You can't put them all in a category and call it truth. No more than men can put women in one category."

"You're right, of course, Bea. So, OK, let's give this thing a whirl," laughed Judith.

Trinity suddenly stepped back and shouted, "Voila!" and handed Judith a mirror.

Judith looked at herself in dismay. "Oh dear Lord. I look like I should be dancing on Bourbon Street."

"Don't knock it," said Trinity mysteriously, chuckling.

"Wait! You didn't! Were you an exotic dancer, Trinity?" asked Lola, not knowing whether to be shocked or to celebrate.

"No, I wasn't," laughed Trinity, "But I'm not dead yet!"

"She's kidding, Lola. As her big sister, I would have chased her down Bourbon Street if I'd ever caught her strutting her stuff on a stage," said Dawn emphatically. Then added, "Besides, you're no slut, Trinity. That's Lola's specialty!"

The sistahs were all laughing hard now when Helen reminded them, "Alright, cut it out. Bitsy's in a hurry!"

Bitsy directed Judith to stand in front of a blank, white door to take photos and started playing fashion photographer. She shouted directions like, "Oh, that looks great, give me another one like that," and "OK, now give me a sexy pout!"

"Sexy?" asked Judith. "I don't want them to be sexy!"

"She means pretty, dear," said Bea, with a reproving glance to Bitsy.

Judith actually did look rather pretty in the photos. The makeup did its magic on camera and made her look nice for the photoshoot.

Bitsy looked at the pictures. "OK, that's it. We've got some good ones. I'll leave my computer here for a little while, Judith, and come back for it later. You can go through and pick out the shots you want and then fill in the online dating site form. But now, I gotta get back to work and back to Lillian. Yuck." Bitsy left her laptop open and made to leave for the museum.

"Wait up, Bitsy, I'll walk out with you. See y'all later. I can't be late," said Lola. They both took off down the street.

Judith looked at all the pictures and then at the dating site. Feeling overwhelmed, she said, "This is never going to work. Let's just forget the whole thing. Actually, let's forget about a man completely. I think I'll just get a dog."

Dawn exclaimed, "Oh my God, I was just talking to Trinity about getting a dog! Let's go find one together."

"I think Judith was kidding," said Helen.

"Well, I'm not!" pouted Dawn.

While the sistahs were talking, Bea walked nervously around the room, occasionally glancing out the front window. Then she swung the computer to face her and started a google search. After finding what she was looking for, she took out her phone and made a few notes on it. Finished, she glanced at the time and, startled at how late it was, jumped up saying, "Oh dear, I have an appointment shortly. Let me run to the ladies real quick, and then I have to leave."

"OK girl, see you in a minute," called Dawn, leaning over to look at the dating site on the computer and instead found Bea's search results. Her eyes widened. "What's this? Look at what Bea was looking up!" she said out loud.

The sistahs gathered round. Trinity asked, "What is it? You look stunned."

Dawn gulped, "This is a website on how to become a minister."

"What?" asked Judith, puzzled. "Why in the world would Bea be looking at that?"

"Maybe she's thinking of ways to make Dawn clean up her act," said Lola, grinning.

"Hah. Funny," sniffed Dawn. "But, you know, it makes sense really. Bea is almost like a guiding force already. She's deeply spiritual, and she ministers to all of us." Then her eyes widened, and she said enthusiastically, "Oh, but this is great! Now we have a romance-finding mission with Judith and a minister mystery with Bea!"

CHAPTER 7

A male voice suddenly boomed from the front door. "Hello, ladies!"

"Who in the world is that?" whispered Dawn.

"That's Jim," said Bea, coming out of the ladies room all business-like, waving at the man. She quickly gathered her belongings and walked across the gallery floor towards him.

"Who is Jim? Your plumber? A new dance partner?" asked Dawn, bewildered and looking at her other sistahs for answers, but they were equally puzzled.

"No, dear, Jim is . . .uh, my new friend."

"Your friend? Really?' Dawn looked around skeptically, then added, "He's a pretty cute friend."

Bea blushed, and Jim did too. "Bea, I think you have some explaining to do," whispered Helen, looking perplexed.

Jim came up alongside Bea. She said, "I was just coming outside to meet you, uh, Jim. But now that you're here, these are my friends, the Gumbeaux Sistahs themselves. Here's Dawn, Judith, and Trinity." Bea looked like she was enjoying the stunned look on her friends' faces, but uncomfortable at the same time. She had been a widow for thirty years, and before this moment, none of the sistahs had thought much about Bea finding another man—much less a handsome one. Yet, here he was with a big, friendly smile on his face and a dog by his side.

"And this is Sunshine," he said, pointing to the grinning, white bulldog. "She's friendly—just a little slobbery." His laugh was huge and deep.

"Well, let's get her outside, shall we?" said Bea, making a beeline for the front door before anyone could ask any more questions. "Bye, dears. I'll see you later," she called.

"Oh yes, you will," said every one of the sistahs, gaping at her retreating back. The couple walked outside and sat on the Friendship Bench in front of the gallery, deeply engaged in conversation.

Dawn swung on Helen immediately, "Helen, what do you know about this?"

"Absolutely nothing," she answered, shrugging her shoulders. "This is all new to me. Bea talks to me most of the time, but you know her. If she wants to keep something to herself, she's like the Sphynx. But she's up to something for sure."

Four women peered out the front window and stared as their friend talked to the good-looking dog and her owner.

"Are you up for a little heart-stretching, dear?"
- Bea

CHAPTER 8

Helen was quiet and deep in thought. She had been handing little makeup brushes to Trinity during the makeup session and then helped Bitsy while she directed Judith's photo shoot. After they finished and Bea left with Jim, she said, "You know, all this talk about love, and now seeing Bea with a new glow around this man has given me an idea. It's been a long time since I've given a workshop. But I was thinking I could offer one right here at the gallery. Maybe a workshop on love for the over forty crowd. What do you think?"

Trinity looked over at Helen. "Sounds intriguing! What would a workshop like that look like?"

"I think I would cover the different kinds of love. I'd have to start with learning to love ourselves. We're always so busy taking care of everyone else that sometimes self-care goes out the window."

"So true," said Lola, nodding.

"I'm guilty of that," said Judith.

"Then I could move right into romantic love. Then love of a higher being or God. Then love of humanity. Maybe wrap it all up with the love of sistahhood!"

"Well, count me in," said Dawn. "That sounds like you're onto something," She turned to Trinity, "Helen gives the best workshops. She's trained in so many different fields—nutrition, spiritual care, meditation, essential oils, and massage—that you can't help but learn so much. You'd love it, Trinity."

"OK, I'm in in too," said Trinity. "And you know I'll help talk it up."

"I'll have to ask Bitsy's help with a PowerPoint presentation to go with the workshop. She helped me last time. That girl knows her stuff. And I'd like to serve gumbo for lunch, of course."

"What will you call the workshop?" asked Dawn.

"I'm not sure. It has to be a name that says something about Louisiana woman—and love."

"Oooh, I've got a name for you," said Trinity. "How about: The Roux to My Heart?'"

"Ha! Cute!" said Helen.

They all chuckled. Judith said, "No, no, wait—how about: I'll Stand Bayou?'"

The sistahs cracked up. Trinity said, "Here's one: Finding Love in Louisiana—A Snoball's Chance in Hell!'"

The sistahs were holding their sides at this point, laughing. Helen shook her head at their craziness, obviously enjoying the sistahs' humor.

"Wait, I've got the winner," said Dawn. "You have to call it: Andouille-ing my Bra!'" The sistahs howled and Helen joined in, gasping, "You three are hilarious. Useless, but hilarious!"

"We're so busy taking care of everyone else that sometimes self-care goes out the window."

-Helen

CHAPTER 9

After the makeup session Dawn, Trinity, Judith, and Helen piled into Dawn's car so she could drive Judith to her house and Helen to her parked car near Judith's place.

"Well, shoot, I'm all fixed up and nowhere to go!" laughed Judith. "It seems a shame to just go home and waste this gorgeous makeup job." She was only kidding. She was itching to scoot home, wash her face, and get her hands on the load of half-finished painting commissions at her studio.

Dawn had the keys halfway to the ignition when she suddenly slapped her open hand to her forehead. "Oh my goodness, she's absolutely right, don't you think, Trinity? Helen? She shouldn't waste this!" She looked meaningfully at her sistahs.

"Of course! That's so true," nodded Trinity. "What should we do?"

"Yeah, where can we go?" asked Helen, agreeing in earnest.

"What are you talking about now?" asked Judith, suddenly on alert and concerned, and with good reason. *Will I ever learn to keep my mouth shut around these women?*

"You know," said Helen, looking thoughtfully out of the window, "It has always occurred to me while shopping at Acquistapace's Market that their gourmet cheese section is like a guy-magnet. I mean, it attracts women too because they have some amazing cheeses in there. But I always see a lot of men in there looking around and sampling their way from the Gouda to the Parmigiano. Ooh, I'm making myself hungry!"

Both Trinity and Dawn turned to look with surprise at sweet Helen in the backseat. "Helen," said Trinity, "You little matchmaker you! That's an absolutely perfect idea!"

"Yep, off we go," laughed Dawn, starting the car.

"Wait, what? You're not serious!" protested Judith.

Dawn took off down the street, laughing, "Serious as a Stilton!"

Trinity giggled, "Earnest as an Edam!"

"Grave as a Gruyere!"

"Solemn as a Sharp Cheddar!"

"Heartfelt as a Havarti!"

"Stop—as in STOP!" laughed Judith. "Do you really expect me to hang out in a cheese aisle trying to pick up men? Do you not know me at all?"

"Well, yes, we do expect you to because it's a damn good idea," said Dawn.

"Yeah girl, we sure do," said Trinity firmly.

Dawn pulled up in front of the grocery store and waited for Judith to get out of the car. She exited slowly looking at her friends with disbelief. Dawn rolled down the window and yelled out, "Go get cheesy with it, sistah!" Judith could hear the three of them giggling in the car.

Judith called back dryly, "You do realize that my house is only a block away from here, right? I'm just going to walk home."

"Now don't do that! Go on —take a chance!" smiled Helen, shrugging. "If nothing else, you'll go home with some great cheese."

"Hey Judith, it looks like we kidnapped you, yet again!" said Dawn. "We know how you hate that. In fact, you . . . camembert it!" She could hear them roaring with laughter as they drove away.

Judith considered just heading home, but started thinking about all that delicious cheese and decided she would like to bring some home.

"Oh, what the heck! I might as well try this ridiculous idea," she thought to herself with a chuckle. *"After all, I almost never look this good. It would be a shame to waste all this beauty!"* She walked into the grocery's front door and realized, *"Besides, I think I'm out of toilet paper, and there's just no arguing with that."*

Inside the store, she headed to the cheese department where at least a dozen different cheeses were being offered as samples in metal-covered containers. Toothpick holders were placed near each sample. It was late morning, so the store had a decent crowd, and many people were sampling, including several nice-looking men in her age range.

She stood in front of one of the sample containers and struggled with the large, heavy purse in her arms and with opening the top of the container, which was slightly stuck. She heard a male voice behind her say, "Here, let me show you how to do that."

Before she could even turn around, Judith was already fuming. She said sarcastically, "I'm sorry, but did you say that you want to show me how to do this?" She whirled around to meet a pair of smiling, brown eyes. Those deep, beautiful eyes were almost enough to stop her anger from building, but not quite. "Do I seriously look like I don't know how to work the cheese? For that matter, does anyone not know how to work the cheese?" She was miffed. She could not tolerate mansplaining on her best days.

He looked amused but took a step back, "Work the cheese?" he laughed slightly. "How does one 'work' cheese?" Then he smiled and said, "Sorry, I didn't mean anything. I was just trying to help."

Judith's first reaction to his laughter was a rising desire to poke him in the eye with her cheese toothpick. But she suddenly remembered the sistahs chiding her about not giving any guy a chance. True, it was a weird thing for him to say, but she could tell he just wanted to be friendly and was, perhaps, flirting with her a little. With a bit of difficulty, she decided that she would give him a second chance to make a first impression. She calmed down and tried to smooth things over with a little bit of humor borrowed from the sistahs.

"Oh well," she said and smiled at him. "I'm sorry too. I didn't mean to be rude—well maybe a little, I did. But I'm sure you could work the cheese as well as anyone." She was blathering, but she muscled on. "I'm . . . I'm sure you'd be very Gouda at it."

He looked at her strangely for a moment. "Well, OK, I'll leave you to it then." He started to move to the next sample container.

Judith sighed with disappointment and disgust. *What did I just say? Ugh, why isn't this easier? I am so out of practice.* She started to walk away, but when she got to the end of the aisle, she turned and gave him one last look. She caught him smiling slightly at her. Blushing like a teenager, she hurried around the corner.

Judith bumbled out of the store and walked the single block to her house, thinking of that smile and how she had seen a lot of humor and kindness in those nice brown eyes.

"I'm really bad at this!" she thought. *"It's a good thing I left. That was possibly the exact opposite of a meet-cute story. Is there such a thing as a meet-awkward story?"*

"Still," she thought with a sigh, *"He was cute. Dammit!"*

She got out her keys, let herself in the house, and stopped short in the foyer. "And dammit again!" she said out loud, "I forgot the toilet paper!"

CHAPTER 10

That night as Judith lay in bed, a prayer of gratitude came to mind. *"Lord, there are many kinds of love in the world and, thanks to you, it's been my great honor in this life to have sampled many and even feasted on a few. It never gets old, does it, Father? Thanks for inventing love. It's probably your best thing. As ever—your will be done. Good night, Father. I love you and I'll see you tomorrow."*

CHAPTER 11

Later that night, Dawn sat on the big, comfy sofa in her den, her laptop propped on her legs, her feet up on the coffee table, and her mind in a bit of a funk. She was tired, but she could not make herself sleep.

Ever since she had accidentally challenged Rocky to a gumbo cook-off, she had been lying awake nights. Getting caught issuing that challenge was horrible, and she still had not replied to his acceptance of her challenge. But she could not stop thinking about how Rocky had called her that old nickname—The Badass of Breaux Bridge. That had hurt terribly and was still making her blood boil with anger. True, she had earned that nickname, but it certainly was not by choice. She had been forced into it. And it was partially Rocky's fault that it had happened.

Dawn and her siblings had endured teasing and bullying growing up after their mom had passed. They had been poor as church mice and were forced to wear other families' hand-me-downs for years. The kids at school could not give that a pass. With their father's physical challenges and his working all the time, it was left to Dawn, the oldest, to take care of her siblings, the meals, and the house. It was too much for a young girl, but Dawn had given it her all. But her all had not been enough to stave off the teasing. So, little by little, Dawn had taken to answering the bullying with her fists. She had defended both herself and her brothers and sister several times, and had earned a bit of a reputation.

But to hear Rocky Breaux use that nickname was just too much. He and Trinity had been such good friends, and Rocky would spend almost every afternoon after school at their house. Dawn had treated him like a little brother. She thought of him that way too.

She could not quite get over hearing those words come out of his mouth.

She glanced towards the Facebook page open on her laptop which showed his smiling photo. When she first reconnected with Rocky, she was proud to learn that he had gone on to become a chef and had done well in his field.

"Why did he have to grow up to become such a putz?" she asked herself. She took the cursor arrow on the Facebook screen and poked him in the eye and then up his nose. The childishness of it made her laugh a little, but it did not relieve her hurt.

"Him and his 'Oh my gravy!'" she grumbled aloud. "I'd like to 'Oh my gravy' his little butt!"

An idea stole into her mind, and it caused a mischievous little grin at the corner of her mouth. She mulled it over and realized that what she needed was to get the whole thing out of her system. She needed to blow off steam at Rocky and reclaim her reputation as a fantastic cook. Her decision was made in that moment and she just went for it.

She typed in a new post on his page.

"Rocky, I was amazed to find you teaching a gumbo cooking class at NOSOC. You couldn't cook your way out of a paper bag. My mom's gumbo recipe would put anything you could scrape together to shame. Re: our gumbo cook-off challenge—you're on. I'll name the time and place—details to follow. Oh-my-gravy that, you little worm!"

Grinning at the sheer spitefulness of it, she let her finger hover over the Post button, then pressed it with a vengeance. She laughed and thought about how she would tell the sistahs in the morning. She could already hear Bea saying, *"Now, dear, was that nice?"* And, of course, Lola would never let her live it down.

"No, it wasn't nice, Bea" smirked Dawn out loud. "But it sure was fun."

The following morning, the phone woke Dawn from sleep. It was Trinity, of course, calling about her Facebook post. The word was out already.

"No, it wasn't nice, Bea. But it sure was fun."

- Dawn

CHAPTER 12

Helen hung up the phone with Bitsy, who was leaving her house early for work, and her face showed her disappointment from their conversation. It had gone something like this:

"Oh Helen, I know I've helped you with your PowerPoint presentation for your last workshop, but please believe me, I'm just too swamped right now to work on it. Lillian has got me crazy! I'm working late and going in early almost every day. She's been absolutely nuts with the events coming up and laying into me constantly. I don't even know what she's so crazy about this. I'm the one doing all the work! I've spoken to her about getting a new assistant for me. She knows I need one. But she says that the museum can't shell out the money right now. I think she's trying to make up for some of the money it cost the museum when they hired her little boy-toy, Thomas. Of course, that was her fault, but thank goodness that's all over with!"

Lillian Deslattes had been chairwoman of the board at the Covington Art Museum for many years. She had fired Judith and put the museum through a terrible time after she had hired Thomas McCann to take Judith's place. Thomas was caught stealing from the museum and was now spending his time in prison. But since then, Lillian had been on a mission to make reparations for her affair with Thomas. She badly needed to make it up to her husband, Jack, and to the museum itself for all the trouble and expense it had caused. Unfortunately, it was Bitsy who was feeling the big pinch from Lillian's mission.

"Oh Bitsy, I'm so sorry Lillian is on a rampage," said Helen sympathetically.

"I know, I'm hung out to dry over here," said Bitsy, grabbing her car keys. "Something's got to give, and soon. I've got to find a way to relieve some of this stress! But don't worry—I'm working on something that might help. I'll tell you about it when I have time."

"Oh shoot, Bits, if you can't help me, who can I get to do this PowerPoint thing? Any ideas? My workshops go so much smoother with them."

"Well, have you tried the high school? They might help you hire a student, and it probably wouldn't cost you too much either."

"Hmmm, not a bad idea. OK, I'll give them a call."

"Alright girl, gotta run, let me know how it turns out."

As soon as they hung up, Helen looked up the high school's number and called the office. She was directed to Molly Smith, Head of the Guidance Counseling Office. Helen told her what she was looking for, and Ms. Smith looked through her student work files. Then she said, "Oh, well, there may be one person, but I'm not sure if he will do. I probably shouldn't even recommend him."

"Wait, does he know PowerPoint? Is he good with computers?"

"They're all good with computers," laughed Ms. Smith. "But he really is a whiz."

"Well, what's the problem? "

"I'm afraid we've a few behavioral problems with Cooper."

"What sort of problems?" asked Helen worriedly.

"Well, off the records, he's been in several fights—in and outside of the school. He has this attitude, and it gets him into trouble. His family situation is not exactly ideal either."

"Is he violent?" asked Helen, then added realistically, "Would I be in danger?" She had had a lifetime's share of violent males. Her ex-husband, Luke, had used her as a punching bag for years before Bea had saved her.

"Oh no," said Molly. "I don't think so. Of course, there was that one time . . . "

"Oh shoot," said Helen. "Isn't there anyone else?"

"There really isn't right now," said Molly. "Not with his skills and not someone who has signed up with our department looking for work."

Helen gulped, "Well, maybe the boy and I could just meet in your office for an interview and see how it goes. Maybe tomorrow afternoon?"

"OK, if you'd like. I can set that up."

"OK, great," said Helen and hung up. "Oh brother," she said out loud. "What am I getting myself into now?"

CHAPTER 13

Judith lay in her bed that night thinking back over her day and appreciating her friends and what they were trying to do for her. A prayer came to mind.

"Dear Lord, I thank you for another day in this beautiful world, and I truly would like to be pleasing to you while I'm here. I thank you, Father, for my children. And my friends. And for art. Your gifts to me have been amazing." She hesitated then added, *"And Lord, if it be your will, please send a new love into my life. As always—your will be done. I love you, Father. Goodnight and see you tomorrow."*

CHAPTER 14

Rocky Breaux stood in front of his gas stove at the New Orleans School of cooking, stirring up a batch of his famous Gumbo Rice. He liked to serve this rice instead of plain white rice with his gumbo. It added just a touch more flavor to the dish. As Rocky put it, *"Man this will put the gris gris on it!"*

Rocky started cooking as a child back in Breaux Bridge, and he knew it was the little details, like using fresh ingredients and the right seasonings, that made all the difference in whether a dish was just good, or truly memorable. Making his food memorable made Rocky himself memorable and had brought him success and popularity in New Orleans. He was invited to many celebrity chef events, and his book, *Rocky Cooks*, was a big seller with the New Orleans foodie crowd.

It had taken many years, tenacity, and a great deal of struggle to make Rocky who he was today. He had been head chef at two local, classic restaurants before landing the head chef job at The New Orleans School of Cooking just a few years ago. Now, at fifty-seven, he was a ball of energy and still going strong.

Coming out of rural Breaux Bridge as a gay, Cajun, small-statured young man who had been bullied for so many years, he felt he had found heaven when he had arrived in New Orleans. There he was accepted, and his food and personality were celebrated.

The two things he had held onto from his old hometown was his deep Cajun accent and his dear, old friend, Trinity. He thought of her now and smiled to himself, *"Thank God for Trinity."*

He had been terribly bullied at their grammar school and so had Trinity's whole family. When Dawn fought back against the bullies who harassed her family, she had defended Rocky a time or two as well. That was how she had gotten that nickname. Rocky had actually liked the name. He often wished he had a cool nickname like that. It never occurred to him that Dawn might be upset by it. It had truly surprised him when she got angry with him the other day in class. He had been so happy to see her, and was teasing her like just like in the old days. But then she suddenly turned on him.

Trinity had assured him that Dawn was not really upset with him, that she was upset for another reason. But he knew his Trinity. She was pretending in order to protect both of them.

Then, after Dawn issued her late-night Facebook challenge to him for a gumbo cook-off, he knew he was right. He had upset her. He had not meant to. He loved their family.

But when he read the Facebook post, he could not help but get angry himself. After all the years he had spent working hard to elevate his skills and reputation, she had tried to shoot him down publicly on social media. She might as well have screamed from the top of the Monteleone Hotel, "Rocky Breaux can't cook!" She was attacking his very way of living. He thought sadly, *"Oh no, chérie, that's the one thing I can't let you get away with."*

What was she thinking? Hadn't he contributed to their family when he was kid? True, they had allowed him in their home, and Trinity had been his pal, but Rocky had tried his best to help out. After their mom died, he was worried that everyone, in their grief, might forget to feed their cute dog, Beignet, so he took it upon himself to take good care of him. And he had done his best to keep Trinity's spirits up when grief and sadness overwhelmed her. When their family's old clothes needed mending, or a button went missing, he did not think that Dawn even realized that it was Rocky who took needle to thread in Trinity's room as they watched Dr. Who after school. He even ironed the clothes after he had finished mending them.

Rocky's mother had been close friends with Trinity's mom, who had been very kind to Rocky before she passed. When she died, Rocky took it hard too. His own parents, while basically good people, both worked long hours and were just absent. He was an only child and felt a terrible loneliness at an early age. But Trinity's mom, and then Dawn, had welcomed him as one of their own. The idea that Dawn would turn on him cut him to the quick. He almost felt as if he were losing his family all over again. And then she insulted his food—his life blood. That made him feel as if Dawn thought him still the down-trodden little kid from their poor, old neighborhood. So, he would accept her gumbo challenge, using his own mom's tried-and-true recipe to prove to her that the little kid had grown up to be someone, just as she, herself, The Badass of Breaux Bridge, had.

1975—Breaux Bridge

Rocky was twelve years old and running for his life. He was supposed to be meeting Trinity at her house after school, but he could not get there without giving away his hideout behind the school's big garbage dumpster. He ducked into that dark spot as soon as he could. It was a secret place he had used more than once, and it served him well. He could not afford to let it be discovered now.

The schoolyard was emptying when he heard them calling his name, "Rocky Raccoon, we know you're in there!"

He felt a cold chill go straight up his back as he recognized the voice of Bobby Busharello and his cronies. Bobby was in the same grade and about the same size as Rocky, which is to say that he was slight and short. Bobby wanted to do serious harm to Rocky's body—maim, disable, and cause excruciating pain. Rocky suspected that without his cronies, Bobby would not be so eager to visit violence upon him. His size might fail him in a fight. But because he had the physical backup of his friends, he could be assured of a victory.

His thug companions egged on the attacks by calling Bobby and Rocky "The Twins" since they were so alike in stature. They even had the same buzz haircuts. The comparison made Bobby feel he had something to prove.

"C'mon out, Twin Rocky," called Bobby in a sing-song voice. "We've got something for you!" Wicked laughter accompanied their calls, and Rocky could tell there were three of them, and that they were close by.

Bobby called out, "Rocky, man, you know we're twins. Why would you be scared of me?"

The other reason they wanted to kill Rocky was that they sensed, even at the age of twelve, that Rocky was different. He was timid and only seemed to like hanging out with girls—Trinity especially. To their way of thinking, Rocky was different, and that was just wrong somehow, and it had to be made right. This theory made sense to their twelve-year-old minds. Unfortunately, it still makes sense to some undeveloped adult minds too.

Suddenly, Rocky felt himself snatched backwards by his shirt collar and hauled out of his hiding place. He landed on his rear on the hard concrete in front of Bobby and his three friends.

Bobby grinned at him, "Now, Rocky, I know they call us twins, but we're not alike, man. Not at all—you know that, don't you?"

Rocky nodded his head truthfully. He could not agree more. "That's right. One of us is smart," he said. He bit his lip and wished he could take that last crack back as soon as it left his lips. Rocky's smart mouth was forever getting him in trouble.

Bobby squinted and looked at Rocky with a snake-like stare. "That *is* right," he said. "And if I was you, I'd know better than to keep talking right now. I guess that makes me the smart one."

His friends laughed, and Rocky just stared at the three of them. He looked around desperately for a chance to run, but, unfortunately, he was not very fast. And as luck would have it, Bobby was the school track star. His two muscular friends were not fast either—or smart. But they sure were strong. Rocky did not stand much a chance at escape.

"So, I'm afraid I have to do something to make us not look like twins anymore. It's the only solution."

"What do you mean?" asked Rocky, genuinely scared now and sweating as Bobby advanced towards him.

Without warning, Bobby hauled off and socked Rocky straight in the mouth before Rocky could even raise his hands in defense. Then again with the other fist, Bobby hit Rocky in the same spot.

Rocky howled as blood spurted, and the terrible pain in his face almost made his knees buckle. Instead he put both hands over his mouth and found the nerve to run. Desperation helped him make it out of the side gate where he glanced behind him to see Bobby and his friends still standing by the dumpster, howling with laughter. To some people, violence is humorous.

Rocky ran all the way to his closest safe place, Trinity's house, and burst in the front door. Dawn and Trinity took one look at him, and Trinity's mouth dropped open and she wailed and started bawling. Dawn hurried him to the bathroom sink and let him rinse his mouth with water, then got a cold wet washrag to help stop the bleeding. After he had rinsed, he looked up hesitantly at himself in the mirror to find that he was missing half of one of his two front teeth. He gasped in horror, and Trinity started crying all over again.

"Who did this?" asked Dawn, her voice calm as ice.

Through tears and shame, Rocky blurted out that it was Bobby Busharello. He told Dawn how Bobby said that he was doing this so that they would not look like twins anymore.

Something dark and dangerous came into Dawn's eyes. She told Trinity to call Rocky's mom, and in the meantime, she had Rocky tell her everything that had happened. When Rocky's mom picked him up, she drove him straight to their dentist. Then Dawn told Trinity that she would be back in a little while.

About an hour later, Dawn came strolling back into the house and washed her hands in the bathroom sink. She called Rocky's number and got him on the phone. He answered with a bit of a lisp and told her that, yes, Bobby had indeed knocked his tooth out. The dentist could fix it though, and he had another appointment in the morning that should take care of it.

"Good," said Dawn. "And Rocky, just between you and me—don't worry about Bobby anymore. Until the dentist fixes that tooth of yours, you two look like twins again."

CHAPTER 15

Helen waited after school with Molly Smith in the high school guidance counselor office. While they waited, Molly filled her in on a few details about Cooper Landry, the student who might be able to help Helen with her workshop computer needs.

"He is the go-to computer guy in the school. If any of the people in the office have a tech problem, we call on Cooper. But . . ." She hesitated and looked over her large black glasses at Helen, "Miss Helen, this is between you and me, but I feel like I need to tell you this before he comes. Cooper's mom died, and his stepdad has not exactly been the father-of-the-year. Rumor has it, he drinks and disappears for long periods of time. The neighbors have heard shouting from the house and have called the police several times. But the stepdad always puts on a good act, and Cooper backs him up for some reason, all just long enough to keep Social Services from placing Cooper in a home

"Oh no," said Helen, her heart softening with sympathy for the boy.

"But because of all that, Cooper has developed, shall we say, a bit of an attitude. He can be pretty hard to take."

"I see," said Helen. She did not know exactly what to expect but decided to just play it by ear. She would give him a chance. She really needed his help.

"And there's more," said Molly, sighing. "We sent him out on one job recently. It was over at the bank down the street. I'm afraid he lasted only half a day before he told the manager to stuff his money where the sun don't shine—but in more graphic terms."

Helen could not help but let out a small giggle, then quickly put her serious face back on and nodded. "I'll bet that went over well at the bank."

"It did indeed," said Molly, with a firm set to her mouth. Then she smiled slightly, "But you know, that bank manager had to admit that before the blow-up, Cooper had finished up the job in about a half-hour while his staff had been wrestling with the problem for days. When I say Cooper is the best at what he does, I really mean it."

There was a loud knock at the door, and a young man with reddish, messy hair and an old, black t-shirt that just said "NO" on it walked in and plopped down in an empty chair next to Helen. He glared first at Molly then turned it on Helen.

"I'm not gonna work on anything stupid," he said. "No data input. Any idiot can do that. Also, I got a job during the week washing dishes at the Beck-n-Call, so I can't work at the same time."

Molly started in, "Now, Cooper, say hello to Miss Helen . . ."

"Hello, Cooper," said Helen, holding out her hand to him.

"No need to shake," he said, keeping his hands to himself. "I can see you right there." He paused looking at her. Then his expression changed slightly and he nodded and mumbled, "Hello."

"Miss Helen is thinking of hiring you for a job she needs done. Maybe you could tell Cooper a little about the work?" she nodded encouragingly at Helen.

Helen turned towards the boy. "Of course. Cooper, I'm going to host a workshop in town, and I need help with putting together a PowerPoint presentation for it. Are you familiar with that?"

Cooper rolled his eyes. "Pretty much any idiot could do that," he mumbled, looking at his feet.

"Well, not this idiot," smiled Helen, "So what I was thinking is this—we could meet at the Gumbeaux Sistahs Gallery after school a few times to work on it. It's not far from here on Columbia Street— do you know it?"

"I can find it. What's it pay?"

Helen thought for a moment and then said, "I can pay twelve dollars an hour, would that be OK?"

"That's pretty generous, I'd say," said Molly.

"But you ain't the one doing the job," he told her dismissively. He turned back to Helen, "I make almost that much washing dishes, make it at least fifteen dollars."

"Are you worth it?" she asked with a shy smile.

"Lady, I'm the best," he said, no smile.

"Well, OK I think I can manage that," said Helen.

"And I want eight hours guaranteed, no matter what happens."

That sounded ominous, and Helen felt a little flustered. She shrugged, "Well, OK, sure. So, would you like to give this a go? We could give it a try to see if we can work together." She said this pointedly, but added, "I really could use some help."

Cooper, who had been examining the ceiling, lowered his gaze and looked straight into Helen's eyes, "Depends. What's the workshop about?"

That surprised both Helen and Molly, "It's about love."

"Aw man," said the young man. "It knew it would be something stupid."

"I'm not gonna work on anything stupid."

- Cooper

CHAPTER 16

After taking care of her landscaping clients for the day, Lola hurried back to her house and showered just in time to greet Bud at the door. He had just driven in from his New Orleans nursery business to spend an evening with her. She was planning on grilling steaks and throwing together a salad, and he was bringing a favorite Pinot Noir. He also picked up a wicked cheesecake from the Italian restaurant next door to his business.

She opened the front door fresh from the shower, her hair still damp and wearing a soft, mint-green sweater and jeans.

They had been dating again for six months now, and it almost felt as if it were for the first time. People who did not know their story and saw them together took them for a new couple and not as a couple who had once been married and divorced over thirty years ago. Things had been going well, but they had run into a hitch. A dark cloud had been forming, and it had to be dealt with.

After a quick dinner, Bud sat his long, lanky self on her purple couch, and Lola knew they had a serious talk ahead of them that evening.

She brought him a glass of wine and joined him on the couch. "Bud, you know we can't ignore this problem anymore. And you know I love you, but this will never work. We just can't do this. Our family and friends will never stand for it. We brought them too much pain our first time around. It will just turn out miserably." She was trying to be reasonable, but her eyes held a deep sadness.

"I know," he said, his eyes looking down into his glass, "I just don't see how to do this either. Too much time has passed."

She said softly, "It might be better for everyone if we just backed off seeing each other."

He looked stunned and reached for her hand. "Well, damn. I didn't expect that," was all he said.

Tears were in Lola's eyes. "I'll miss you, Bud. I really will."

"I guess it's the right thing to do. Our friends and family mean so much to us, and we're not exactly young anymore, to be acting this way."

"Speak for yourself," Lola grinned momentarily, but her eyes still brimmed with sadness.

"I guess you're right. We have other people to consider—my family, and yours, and all our friends."

"Your children alone have to be considered in this," said Lola. Bud had grown children with his second wife, Susan.

"Everything was different when we were younger and could get away with anything," she laughed softly.

"So, we both agree? We need to do this, right? It seems such a shame."

"Yes, I think we do."

"Will you be OK?" he asked, concerned.

"Sure," said Lola, wiping away tears that threatened to fall and not meaning her words for a single minute.

CHAPTER 17

On Friday nights, the sistahs often met up at the Gumbeaux Sistahs Gallery for an end-of-the-week glass of wine. They were glad for an excuse to spend time together.

Tonight, Dawn, Lola, Judith, Bitsy, Helen, and Bea were able to make it. They sat with Sistah Sling cocktails in hand, a Gumbeaux Sistahs specialty, and every one of them was staring at Lola, aghast at the bombshell she had just dropped.

Dawn was especially shocked. Her mouth was hanging open as she sputtered, "What do you mean you broke up? Are you serious?"

"I'm afraid so," said Lola. "I mean, we tried, but it became too much. Bud lives in New Orleans, and I live in Covington. It's just too far to keep up a relationship. C'mon, you know long-distance relationships never work. We decided that it was just crazy to keep putting off the inevitable."

"Are you on drugs?" yelled Dawn, getting to her feet. "You two love each other! No, make that *worship* each other!" Suddenly her eyes narrowed, and she looked closely at her friend. "What are you not telling us, Lola?"

Lola just looked at Dawn with a terribly sad expression in her eyes.

Bea interrupted Dawn's tirade. "Dawn, can't you see she's upset? Don't torture her."

"But . . ." said Dawn, pointing at Lola, unable to finish her sentence.

Bea turned to Lola. "We're really sorry, dear. We all liked Bud."

"Yes, we liked him—and she liked him too!" said Dawn, winding up again. "So much so that she was married to the man at one time, and I fully expected her to marry him again. He's perfect for her. I was all set to plan the biggest wedding the Northshore has ever seen!"

Bitsy piped up, "I'm sure Lola knows what she's doing. We should support her decision." She glanced at her watch and said, "Oh for Pete's sake! I'm sorry. I gotta run. I've got some important errands to run this evening." She picked up her purse and waved goodbye on her way out.

"Where is she going in such a hurry on a Friday night?" wondered Dawn. "Everyone is acting so weird today."

"Not sure," said Judith. "But she's been running on all cylinders for a while now. Usually it's Lillian that has her hopping for work, but it's after hours. Still, I'll bet it's Lillian-related."

Helen added wistfully, "I miss having Bits around more."

"But, OK, back to you, Lola," said Dawn, not giving in an inch. "We need to talk about this."

"I really don't feel like talking about it, Dawn," Lola said quietly. "I'm happy to be with y'all tonight, and I really need your support, but could we talk about something else?"

This silenced Dawn who just stared at her friend. The whole business was very odd. She felt terrible for Lola and absolutely furious with Bud for allowing this to happen. She decided to let it go for now, but this was far from over.

To change the subject, Helen told them all about meeting her new employee, Cooper Landry, at the high school. "I'm probably in over my head working with him, but at least he knows his stuff. His counselor says he is head of his class in computer science. They even call on him into the school office when they need techy help. I just hope with his troubled background that we can work together."

"If anyone can, it's you, dear," said Bea. "If you need me to meet him with you, I'd be happy to."

"I'll let you know, Bea. We would just have to make sure our time on the Friendship Bench is covered that day," said Helen.

A few years ago, Helen and Bea had started the Friendship Bench tradition which entailed taking turns sitting and making themselves available on a certain park bench near Bea's house. People who needed someone to talk to showed up, one at a time, to sit on the bench with either Bea or Helen for a half hour on certain days and times of the week. Sometimes people wanted to talk about serious problems, but other times, people just showed up because they were lonely and wanted to talk as if to a friend. Sometimes they discussed divorce, or loss, or their far-away children, and other times they might talk about recipes for pickled shrimp. Neither woman was a trained therapist, but they both knew how to be a friend.

Since its inception, they had added two more benches—one in front of the Gumbeaux Sistahs gallery and another by the pavilion in the nearby town of Abita Springs. Helen and Bea could not cover all the benches, so they had also added several women volunteers to their little organization which seemed to be growing all the time.

"I'll make sure the bench is covered," said Bea.

"In that case, I could use your calm head. This kid is a handful." Helen rolled her eyes.

"Let us know how that goes, Helen," said Dawn. She got up suddenly to grab the pitcher, and refilled everyone's cocktail glasses. While making the rounds she changed the subject "Hey, Judith, remember we talked about the two of us adopting dogs?"

"Yes, I think we mentioned it when my face was being attacked with makeup by Trinity," laughed Judith.

"I was wondering if you'd like to get together tomorrow and talk about what kinds of dogs we might get. I'm going over to the Humane Society tomorrow to look around and see what dogs are available for adoption, and was hoping I could stop by afterwards to talk about it."

"Sure, come on over. I'll be home all day painting and getting ready for my date on Sunday."

For the second time that day, Dawn's mouth fell open. "What? You never mentioned a date!" She literally jumped up and down excitedly.

Watching Dawn's antics, Judith said with a smile, "Gee, wonder why!" Then she added, "Yes, crazy woman, I agreed to meet this man for a cocktail Sunday evening."

"Who is he?"

"He just popped up on one of the dating sites that y'all signed me up for." Judith tried to give the appearance that she was calm about the whole thing, but inside she was plenty nervous—and kind of excited. "He's a local vet from Slidell."

"Do we know him? Slidell is only a half hour away. What's he like? Is he cute?" Dawn was off and running.

"No, we don't know him, and yes, he seems nice so far, and yes, he's kind of cute," answered Judith laughing.

"Good God, Dawn, she won't know anything till she meets him," said Helen impatiently. Then to Judith she said, "Just be careful, sistah."

Dawn suddenly got an evil glint in her eye. "Well, you're probably right, but the minute he gets out of your bed Sunday night, you'd better pick up the phone and call us. Your love life is our project, after all, and so we have a right to know. Besides, I won't be able to sleep."

"No one is getting in my bed except *moi*—and hopefully early, too. We've got a big day at the gallery on Monday. But yes, I'll call you afterwards and let you know what kind of disaster it, no doubt, turns out to be."

CHAPTER 18

L illian Deslattes sat at her desk at the Covington Museum on Saturday morning trying to unstick her stapler. She had tried to staple several invoices together when the machine stuck fast and stubbornly refused to let go of either papers or staple.

"Stupid thing!" she seethed, growing more impatient by the moment. She was already in one of her blacker moods as it was. In the last few months, since that business of letting Judith go from her manager's position at the museum, Lillian would occasionally drop into a raging anger at the thought of the whole nonsensical business. She tried to forget about it, put the whole thing behind her, but she was still very susceptible to the rage.

As Chairwoman of the board, she had orchestrated Judith's release and forced the board, through her strong will and vicious tongue, to replace Judith with the much younger Thomas McCann, with whom Lillian had been having a fling.

But that scheme had backfired horribly on Lillian in ways she could never have imagined. She mused about the disastrous turn of events. "It was *unbelievable. First Thomas turns out to be a thief and goes to jail. Then the museum loses a great employee—thanks to me— plus a great deal of income from our failed Spring-Fling fundraiser. And to top it all off, my husband Jack sleeps with one of those 'Gumbeaux Sistahs'—Lola. Truly unbelievable. You can't make this stuff up!"* She said that last sentence out loud and threw her hands up in the air, adding loudly, "And now this damn stapler wants to eat the office receipts!"

She was working herself up to a boiling point and was sorely tempted to throw the stapler across the room. And so, she did. She was hoping it might loosen the machine and break her out of her dark rage. Her perfectly coiffed dark hair threatened to spring free, and her creamy, light skin was splotched with anger.

She could not get a break. She had only succeeded in putting a gash in the wooden chair where the stapler had hit, which elevated her anger even more.

She blamed much of what had happened on the Gumbeaux Sistahs. She had never gotten along with Judith when she had worked at the museum. They clashed too much over creative control. Then on the night of the Spring Fling event, the sistahs had lured all the museum's guests away to the Gumbeaux Sistah's Gallery opening, costing the museum a great deal of money which they counted on every year. And Lola especially had caused her grief. Lillian and her husband were still patching up their marriage after that horribly hurtful period of disloyalty.

Lillian stared at the ceiling, trying to control her emotions. She gave up on fixing the stapler. Instead of using it to dent chairs, she hurried out of her office and headed over to the Director's office. She would ask Bitsy to fix it. That woman could fix anything.

As she drew closer to the office, Bitsy's telephone voice drifted out and reached Lillian's ears.

"I know, Bea. I can't believe they broke up! How could Lola and Bud do that? I'm actually a little shaken. I think we all are!" Bitsy paused listening, then said, "You're right. This is going to be so hard on them. You and I know they both really love each other. I'm not sure that this is the best thing for them to do. I only hope Lola has given this a lot of thought and knows what she's doing."

Lillian stood in the hall listening to the rest of the conversation. She had been fighting the notion of retaliation on the sistahs for months. It was a battle she was slowly losing. In fact, it was the reason that she made Bitsy work much longer hours than necessary these days—just because it scratched that itch she had for revenge. There really was no reason for Bitsy to be working on a Saturday morning.

There was nothing that could not wait until Monday, but Lillian had insisted just because she could use it to poke at the sistahs in a small, passive-aggressive way.

But what she had just overheard from Bitsy was such a juicy little morsel of information that it tickled Lillian's desire for revenge. With a shiver, Lillian felt herself giving into her darker side. She knew she should not go there, but it felt so good in the moment to consider it. She felt like she had been losing for so long, and she suddenly felt like she could win again. Lillian dearly loved to win. She did not yet know what she would do with the information, but she filed it away in a mental drawer where it was easily accessible.

CHAPTER 19

Dawn parked in front of Judith's house Saturday afternoon and walked up the sidewalk. You could not miss Judith's house if you tried. It was painted yellow with a cornflower blue trim, and she actually had a painting hung outside on the front of the house. It was one of her Gumbeaux Sistahs paintings. The whole house blasted the message, "An artist lives here!"

She noticed that the border of Creeping Jenny stems that lined the sidewalk were looking brown and droopy. Judith was always trying to do something with her yard, but did not usually have much time or luck with it. She said she was bound and determined not to plant grass because she did not want to mow it. It probably would have saved her time and money in the long run if she had just planted the darned grass. These little plants were in trouble, and she would probably have to replant it all.

From out of nowhere, a little, fawn-colored pug suddenly ran up to the browning plants and started digging up some of the remaining border.

"Well, that's not going to help anything," Dawn said, laughing and making shooing motions at the little pup. "Leave that alone! Where did you come from anyway? You're adorable!"

The pug turned and ran up the front steps and barked at the front door.

Dawn followed the dog and rang the doorbell. She leaned over and said, "Wait a minute, pup, is this your house? Did Judith go ahead and get a dog without me? Looks like she got herself a cutie!" The dog spun in circles excitedly as Dawn spoke to it.

Judith came to the front door and opened it. "Come on in. I've got coffee on." She looked down at the dog and said, "Well, hey, Cutie!"

Judith turned to go back into the house, thinking, *"Oh my Lord. Dawn must have gotten a dog today down at the Humane Society. And she got such a cute one! It's kind of odd that she brought it here with her. I guess she just wanted me to see it. Shouldn't it be on a leash?"*

The dog ran inside after Judith, and Dawn followed, saying to the pup, "Where are you going, you pretty thing?"

"It's a girl," said Judith, looking closer.

"Isn't she just the cutest!" said Dawn, helping herself to coffee.

The little pug grabbed the edge of one of Judith's rugs and started doing her best to rip it apart.

Judith thought, *"Uh oh, I don't want to fuss at Dawn's dog. I'll let her handle this. She'll correct her, won't she?"*

The dog immediately ran from the rug over to a potted plant and started sniffing it. Then she jumped up and started digging the dirt out, spreading it all over the kitchen floor.

"Oh my Lord, but you're going to be handful!" said Judith, alarmed now and hoping Dawn would take the hint and step in.

Dawn went into the pantry to get a broom and dustpan to help clean up the dirt. She shook her finger at the dog, "What's to be done with you, little pug?"

Then Dawn and Judith looked at each other and asked at the same exact time, "So what did you name her?"

"What?" they said at the same time—both of them looking completely confused.

Then Judith asked, "Wait—isn't this your dog?"

"No way. I thought it was yours!"

They looked at the bad, little pug and then burst out laughing. They had to hold each other up in the middle of the dirty floor they were laughing so hard. They kept pointing to the dog and then cracking up again.

While they were laughing, the pug jumped up on the kitchen chair and licked at Judith's coffee cup and sugar bowl.

"Holy Moley, whoever this dog is, she's a terrorist!" laughed Dawn.

"She sure is! I wonder where she came from. I've always loved pugs. They're the cutest things, and they obviously have a sense of humor," Judith grinned. "But what in the world should we do with her?"

"Maybe you could just put her back out in the front yard again, and she'll go home."

"We could try that, but it seems kind of iffy," said Judith. "Pugs are kind of expensive, and someone could just snatch her. If we do put her out, maybe we should try following her."

The dog looked up as if she knew she was being discussed, then promptly squatted on the kitchen floor in front of the stove.

"Oh my Lord!" yelped Judith, running for the mop.

Dawn started laughing again, "Seriously, who would want this crazy dog? She's terrible!"

Judith mopped and grinned, "Well, let's see if we can get her home."

They walked outside with the pup and stood there waiting for the dog to ease on down the road, hopefully towards her home. It went immediately to Judith's Creeping Jenny plants and started ripping them up like before.

"Oh no, don't do that!" yelped Judith.

"I don't know. She might be doing you a favor," laughed Dawn. "Those plants are looking pretty sad."

"I know, aren't they?" said Judith. "They're supposed to be hardy, but they're very fragile. Instead of Creeping Jenny, I've started calling them *Creepy* Jenny. All these dead plants are making my place look like a haunted house."

Dawn laughed, and the dog ran up to her, barking joyously. She turned and ran in a circle then up the steps and back into the house.

"You knucklehead!" Dawn yelled after it. "Come back here!"

"You know, Dawn, I'm just realizing as I'm looking at this pup, doesn't she seem kind of dirty and a little roughed-up? Like she's been running loose for a while?"

"Someone probably disowned her. Wonder why?" she smirked.

"I'm gonna give her something to eat then see if I can find her owner."

"I wouldn't, Judith. If you feed this dog, she'll probably never leave you."

"Oh don't be silly. I think she's hungry. I wonder if dogs can eat gumbo. That's all I have in the house."

"OK," said Dawn, heading back inside. "Give me some too, and I'll never leave you either."

CHAPTER 20

"Oh, so that's who Jim is!" laughed Helen. "You could have told me before, you know. The sistahs all have you running off to Bermuda to marry that guy already!"

"I know," said Bea. "But I have a lot of information to gather still, and decisions to make. I didn't want everyone's input until I knew more about it. So, can you meet him with me? I think it might help."

"Of course, see you tomorrow."

"So, this is where it all began," he said, his light blue eyes beaming at Bea. They stood in front of the original Friendship Bench in the park across from Bea's house. He appraised the woman standing next to him in the warm, afternoon sunlight. Unlike most people who met Bea, he was not as easily entranced by her intellect, charm, and charisma. He had met plenty of smart, charismatic people in his field. His white collar and black frock brought him up to many doors of human nature and gave him the keys to unlock their secrets. He needed to be open to her, but also to take her request into serious consideration. But he did like her very much and hoped they could be friends.

"Yes, and here comes Helen," said Bea, waving to her friend. Helen walked up and Bea introduced them. "Father Jim, this is my good friend Helen Hoffmann. Helen—Father Jim Jacobs from Grace Episcopal Church.

He took Helen's hand, "It's so good to meet you, Helen. Bea has been telling me a lot about you. I can't wait to hear more about your story."

"It's so nice to meet you too—and is it OK to call you Father? I wasn't sure of your title."

"Oh sure, people call me Pastor, Father and all sorts of things. Jim is fine too. Episcopalians are pretty flexible on that front. Call me anything you want."

"Oh dear," giggled Helen to Bea, "It's a good thing Dawn's not here. We'd already be in all sorts of trouble."

He grinned at her, "In that case, I'm looking forward to getting to know Dawn, too."

Bea spoke up, "I wanted you to be here, Helen, because the Friendship Bench was started by both of us."

"It's been a wonderful experience, Father Jim," said Helen. The Friendship Bench has helped a lot of people who need to talk to someone, and it helps those that want to listen too."

Bea then told him how they had been inspired by a newspaper story they had seen years ago about something called a Grandmother's Bench in Zimbabwe. "It was all about shared time, talking, and listening to people," she said. "The Friendship Bench is based on the same principle. People take turns on the bench, staying no more than half hour, and logistically it has worked out. And now we have three benches going."

Helen added, "But it could be helping many more people. Some of the people who have come to talk at the bench have become listeners. We have been hand-picking people, little by little, to become volunteers on the benches. Of course, some people are too damaged and in pain to listen, but those people are always welcome to keep talking. It works out."

"It's really impressive, ladies," said Father Jim encouragingly. "The love behind it all is simply God-given. You've achieved something unique and powerful, and I admire you to pieces over the whole idea. Are you sure you want to start in on something new?"

"You mean at my age?" asked Bea, looking him in the eye.

"No, no, of course not," he said, but he looked uncomfortable. "I mean you've done a lot here already."

"You're never too old to start again. It could be the best present you ever give yourself."

"I'll remember that, Bea," he said seriously.

"So, back to the Friendship bench. We think that, with some help, more people could jump in with us. We can't monitor all the benches to make sure people are safe, so we thought we'd ask for help. The church seems to have a couple of followers," she paused to laugh with a tinkle, "So you popped into mind" explained Bea. "To be honest, we talked and prayed about it. I go to your church, and I like you and your sermons, so we thought we'd ask you."

"What would you need from me?" asked the pastor.

"Just your friendship," said Bea, slyly grinning up at him.

"Don't listen to her, Father," laughed Helen. "She's lying through her teeth! We need your social media accounts and your voice to announce what we're doing."

"I don't think I can do that since it's not related to the church," said Father Jim, shaking his head.

Bea went on stubbornly, "So how do I become related to the church?"

"You'd have to become a lay minister."

"That's what I thought. I've been looking into it. OK, fine," said Bea, "Let's do it."

Father Jim looked at the tiny sixty-nine-year-old woman in the little straw hat and shook his head, "I'm afraid it's not that simple and it's really not up to me. Many churches have Lay Ministry programs and those programs come in different forms. Some are more casual, but ours is pretty formal. It sounds like you want to work with the lay ministry, but have your own agenda in mind. I think you'll have to talk to the Bishop to get approval."

"You're never too old to start again. It could be the best present you ever give yourself."

- Bea

CHAPTER 21

On Sunday evening, Judith sat at a back table in Café Rani and waited, sipping at her vanilla latte. The front door opened, and she nervously glanced up, looking for the handsome, white-haired veterinarian from Slidell who had arranged to meet her today for coffee. His name was Winston.

"Winston is such an old-fashioned name," she mused. She wondered what would inspire a mother to name their child something that sounded like it came from the eighteen hundreds. It sounded so courtly, so gentlemanly. Nowadays, they named their little boys Dakota, or Jackson, or even Jaxon, which Judith rather liked.

She noticed that it was already twenty minutes after the time they had agreed to meet. The door opened again, and two women walked in that she recognized as patrons from her old job at the art museum. They stopped to chat at her table, and she was proud to fill them in about the opening of the Gumbeaux Sistahs gallery. She invited them to come and visit sometime, and they seemed delighted by an invitation from the artist and co-owner.

Then it was thirty-five minutes past the agreed-upon time, and she crumbled her napkin, gathered her purse up, and walked out the door.

"Gentleman—my eye," she thought. Then she sighed and said out loud, "Welcome to online dating."

CHAPTER 22

awn was in the back office of the gallery when Judith barged in and plopped down in a chair by the gallery's pastry case where the sistahs sold fresh scones and cookies daily. Dawn stuck her head out from the back, surprised. "What are you doing here? You're supposed to be having wild monkey-sex on your first date with that Winston guy!" She teased until she saw her friend's face.

"I got stood up!" said Judith. "He's never even met me, yet somehow he knew we were incompatible!" She laughed, but she was thoroughly disgusted. "Ah well, probably saved me the trouble of not liking him first."

"I'm sorry, honey. What a jerk!"

"That's so rude, isn't it?" said Judith. "I mean, how hard is it to text someone if you can't or just don't want to make it?"

"Well, you know what they say . . ." began Dawn.

"If you're going to tell me that I have to kiss a lot of frogs before I find a prince—don't bother. I'm so past that. I'm not willing to kiss even one frog, or slug, or amoeba, or any other slimy creature—like a Winston."

"OK, OK. I get it," said Dawn, plunking down in the chair next to her, sighing.

"Dawn, I know I'm not a princess—not anymore anyway," she laughed. "And I don't expect men to have to kiss frogs until they get to me either. I don't feel that, at my age, love should be such a giant, difficult quest. I've had great loves and four babies in my life. I just think it would be nice to experience love one more time, but I want it to be easier this time. It's as simple as that."

"Well, don't give up now," said Dawn. "The Sistahs are taking this project seriously and Trinity will flat kill both of us if you give up on love after one non-date. Just think of it this way; he didn't even show up. Talk about doing you a favor! Can you imagine what a jerk he is if he pulled a stunt like this? You dodged a bullet there. Personally, I don't think this date counted."

Judith looked at her and smiled. "You're so great, Dawn. I wish you were a guy. I'd date you in a minute." She laughed and poked her friend on the arm.

"I know, right?" laughed Dawn. "Can I tell my husband that you propositioned me? Opportunities to make Dan jealous these days are few and far between. In fact," she said, standing, "C'mon. You look fabulous. Let's not waste it. I'm taking you out on a date! Let's go over to the Southern Hotel and hold up their bar. I haven't had a Sistah Sling in too long."

CHAPTER 23

The next afternoon, Judith sat in an Adirondack chair in her backyard, reading a book under the big shady oak tree and watching the little pug run herself crazy. She felt lucky that the yard was fenced in, and she could let the dog run free.

A wooden deck sat in the middle of the yard with a boardwalk leading out to it from the back steps. She had been trying to grow irises in one patch by the deck for a couple of years. The yard was hard to manage. There was no grass, and there was a giant oak tree which provided lovely shade and summer coolness but made it hard to grow anything near it. Not even the iron plants that grew like weeds in neighboring yards did well there. But she had had a little luck with the purple Louisiana iris. She been growing them in one little patch by the side of the deck, and the last blossom was still hanging around on its tall stalk. That small modicum of success she had had, even with the only flower sitting in a small patch of sunlight, was thrilling to her.

Her attention was suddenly torn away from her book as she heard a cacophony of yips and growls coming from underneath the deck. There was obviously a chase going on under there. Suddenly the pug came flying out from beneath the deck, chasing a squirrel who, thank God, was faster than the lightning-speed of the young dog.

But instead of running up a tree, the squirrel dove back underneath the deck, time and again. The pup discovered, to her great joy, that the ground was still wet from rain, and that running in the wet mud under the deck was a treasured experience. She stopped and looked up when Judith shouted, seeing the dog's beautiful, fawn coat covered with dark mud. The pug's look said, *"What? You should try this— it's a blast!"*

Judith chased the dog around the yard trying to catch and wash her, but the little pug eluded her grasp. Calling for the dog to "come" was nothing but a joke.

Then Judith had an idea. She knew the dog liked to chase things, so she called out and got the pug's attention. Then Judith took off running around the corner of the house to the back door and stopped on the steps and waited.

Without hesitation, the dog swung around the corner of house, giving chase. She stopped right in front of Judith with a big grin and plopped the last blooming iris at Judith's feet.

"Oh good Lord. You are really hard on a garden, pup—not to mention on me. Lola would have you banished for being such a landscaping terrorist!"

The dog looked up, panted, and grinned broadly.

"That gives me an idea that's long overdue." Judith turned her back on the pug so it could not see her laughing at its antics, pulled her phone out of her pants pocket, and dialed Lola's landscaping service number.

CHAPTER 24

I f Judith was going to do this, then she might as well get it over with. She was looking forward to it as much as a root canal. Maybe, given a chance, she would actually choose the root canal over this. Maybe if she actually needed a root canal, then she would not have to go through with it at all. Should she pray to need a root canal?

"Oh good Lord. Just go inside, have one cocktail, and give it a try," she told herself, and stepped out of the car into the night air.

She walked to the front corner door of a local watering hole in Covington and pushed the big wooden door open. She chose this place because it served food, seemed safe enough, and had kind of a local, friendly feel to it rather than just some loud bar blaring country music.

When Trinity had called her and made her promise to try this next step in her dating project, she had balked. She truly did not want to go hang out in a bar, for heaven's sake. But Trinity had pointed out that she should try everything in the dating world arsenal at least once on her quest for romance. Judith had told her that she'd think about it. Then at home this evening, she thought she might as well get this over with. Hopefully there would be a friendly group of men sitting together who might in interested in talking to her. That was how it worked sometimes when she was younger.

Of course, back then, she was usually surrounded by her own friends who were cutting up and just out for a fun evening. Tonight, she was solo. Somehow, she could not envision pulling this off with any of her sistahs so she had not mentioned a word that she was doing this tonight to any one of them. Not even Lola or Dawn. She would feel too self-conscious and just clam up because her friends were sure to do all the talking anyway. *"And what good would that do?"* she thought. *"Besides, this way, if I make a fool out of myself, there won't be any witnesses."*

She picked out an empty place at the bar near a tableful of people which included some solo men. That seemed promising. That promise faltered when she walked across the floor to take her seat. She realized to her dismay that not one person in that little group even raised their heads or shifted their eyes to register her presence. The invisible woman had arrived.

But she had half-expected this. She was used to it, truth be told. Being invisible was sometimes the curse of the middle-aged woman. Of course, sometimes it was an advantage too. An invisible woman could get away with things while others could not and they could be more observant in situations than most. People said things around her they would not normally say within earshot. That proved interesting at times.

But tonight, she had hoped for a little more visibility. She had worn heels and a black dress. Her hair looked great and she had felt pretty good when she left the house. *"Oh well,"* she thought. *"I'm giving it a try, and that's all I said I would do."*

So she sipped on the Manhattan she had ordered and thought about going over to the Southern Hotel next time where the crowd might be more sophisticated and accepting of her. *"Or maybe this just isn't such a great way to meet people anymore,"* she thought. She was OK with that. *"It sure isn't a heck of a lot of fun, that's for sure."*

At least her cocktail tasted decent. She relaxed and noticed a group of young women sitting by the front window. They had been there for a while, apparently, and had enjoyed a few drinks—also apparently. Their laughter was loud and growing louder.

One of the women, a twenty-something-year-old, broke from the crowd, probably looking for the ladies room. Stumbling and swaying a bit, she headed straight for Judith, which was confusing. When she got next to her, instead of talking to Judith, she acted as if Judith was not there. The young woman leaned over the bar and hungrily and helped herself to the garnishes that were prepared for cocktails in the bar well. They were not there for bar patron snacks. The woman came away with a whole handful of orange peels. After chomping on a couple of them she made a face and said, "These carrots are terrible." She threw the rest away in a nearby trash can then she went on her way to find the bathroom.

Invisible woman, Judith, shook her head, finished her drink, headed out, and giggled all the way back to her car.

CHAPTER 25

Helen and Bea were just setting up Helen's laptop, and helping themselves to some coffee in the Gumbeaux Sistahs' Gallery, when in walked Cooper wearing worn athletic shoes, old jeans, and a flannel shirt over his usual faded black "NO" t-shirt The first words out of his mouth were, "Who's she?" pointing to Bea.

"'Good morning' might be nice, dear," said Bea, looking the young man over and coming to her feet. She held out her hand. "As in, 'Good Morning, I'm Bea Walker, and you must be Cooper.'"

"Yeah," said the young man, not looking at her and plopping down noisily in a chair. He opened his own computer. "Let's get this over with," he said, sounding bored.

Helen looked at Bea who raised her eyebrows back at her friend. Bea shook her head, "Cooper, Miss Helen here is a very kind person who needs your help. But you should know that I'm not as kind as she is, and I have a rule. Be polite to my friend or hit the road. If you need this job, be nice to her because she's had a rough time in life, and I'm not going to let you give her any more heat. Do we understand each other?"

Helen rolled her eyes and thought, *"Well, that's that! The boy is sure to walk right out the door."*

But to her surprise, he said, "Look, I'm here to get this job done for Miss Helen. The point being—I'm here, aren't I?"

Helen stepped in at this point. "Great. Then let's get to work. Cooper, I've brought you text and photos on this flash drive. What I'm interested in having you do is produce a slide show for me. I can give you the flash drive now and then I'd like you to put it all together. Then we'll meet back and tweak it. And at the workshop, I'd like you to sit in and work the computer for me and make sure all goes well."

"I'm not going to any stupid workshop," he said angrily. "Are you trying to kill me with boredom?"

"Once again, dear," said Bea, "I'm not going to let you run your mouth and hurt my friend. I believe she has spelled out the details of the job very clearly. If the job isn't for you, then so be it. She's paying you decent money and there are others who can do this work. You're creating a slideshow, not hacking into the Pentagon. So, dear, take it or leave it."

Helen laughed and said, "I wouldn't mess with Miss Bea if I was you, Cooper. Look, I'd like for you to do this job. Can you manage it?"

"In my sleep," he mumbled. He had an angry sneer on his face at Bea, but turned to Helen and said, "OK, I need the money, but don't expect any extras. Everyone wants me to do more than I'm hired for. I'm not going to delete your cookies, clean up your hard drive, figure out why you were kicked off Pinterest, or any other stupid thing."

"Rats!" said Helen, laughing. "I actually have been kicked off of Pinterest." She smiled at the boy. "But OK. That's the deal. Shall we meet back next week, and you can show me what you've put together?"

"I'll be here," he sighed. He got to his feet, picked up Helen's flash drive and walked out.

"Well, he's a delight," said Bea, staring after him.

Helen shook her head, "I don't know what's going on with him. He's a bit of a pain in the neck, I know. I don't know why he's so mean, but it makes me feel for him."

"Well, maybe he's the kind that grows on you," said Bea. "Like a fungus."

"I wouldn't mess with Miss Bea if I were you."
- Helen

CHAPTER 26

L ater that night Bud walked into Ruby's Roadhouse in Mandeville, LA. The band had already started playing, so he headed to the bar, ordered an Abita beer, and settled in to listen. He had worked all day at his business, Broussard Nurseries, and had made a special trip across the lake.

He did not really want to be here, but he was lonesome for Lola, so he was glad for the distraction. He had come to hear the female singer. He had heard she was great, and anyway, he wanted to relax from working all day at the nursery.

After a minute of listening to the singer, he thought, *"Wow, she's fantastic!"* The pretty, mocha-skinned singer and her whole band were close to Bud's age and were wailing some of his favorite cover songs, like *Rolling on the River, Midnight Train to Georgia,* and even Aretha's *Respect.* Bud could not keep his feet still and found them tapping along to the beat. During the last song, the singer caught Bud's eye, winked, and smiled at him.

Bud smiled back and nodded. He was enjoying himself much more than he thought he would. He hoped he would get a chance to talk to her, but the group had a while still to go. He would just wait.

Lillian Deslattes was across the street heading into Saia's grocery. She looked up when she heard the loud music coming from the local bar.

At that moment, she was surprised to see Lola's ex-boyfriend, Bud, strolling into Ruby's by himself. *"What's he doing here?"* she thought. Lillian remembered that he lived on the other side of the lake. *"This is a long way to come for an after-work beer. Must be a very good band tonight."*

She stood watching the front door to the bar for a minute before a very "Lillian" sort of idea came into her head. She reached into that drawer in her mind where she filed useful information and pulled out the bit that said Lola and Bud had broken up recently, and that it had not been an easy breakup. Lillian mulled that information over in her mind for a moment. Did she want to stir up trouble? For all the trouble she had caused the sistahs, Lillian actually did have a kind side to her, especially when it came to her husband and family. And it did show its face now and then. But, no, apparently kindness did not want to come out and play tonight. Lillian wanted to play that other sort of game—the kind where she might get a little revenge on Lola for sleeping with her husband, Jack.

Lillian had not forgotten that transgression for a moment and never would. Lillian had suspected Jack of having an affair, but it had come as a complete shock to find out it was with Lola. But Lillian had been having an affair of her own with young Thomas McCann. After Thomas had been arrested and jailed for stealing from the museum, their relationship abruptly ended. Jack found out about her affair at the same time of the arrest, and Lillian had found out about Lola. Since then, she and Jack had come to a rocky truce about their marriage and were still trying to find their footing again.

No, Lillian had not yet forgotten. Or forgiven.

She got through her grocery shopping and put the bags into the trunk of her car. She checked her hair and lipstick in the car's side mirror, then sashayed across the street to the bar.

Pushing open the door, she immediately spied Bud across the semi-crowded room standing at the bar with a beer in his hand. He stood taller than most of the people around him. She thought with a wicked little laugh, *"With his silver hair and lean face, he still looks like a movie star. This is going to be painless."*

The band was taking their first break. There was no one on the stage, but the canned music had been switched on loud. Lillian strode confidently across the floor in time to the heavy bass beat. She felt good and looked good, and she intended to work it in her favor.

"Hi, Bud." She had to speak loudly up at him to be heard. She saw recognition come into his eyes as she dug her phone out of her purse.

"Lillian," said Bud warily with a nod, knowing her past with Lola.

"It's been a while," she said. "I heard you and Lola broke up."

"Word certainly gets around," drawled Bud.

"Well, can't say as I blame you. She's awful. She slept with my husband, you know."

"I heard about it," he said, clearly uncomfortable.

"So, is the band any good?" asked Lillian. "I'm not sure if I should hang around for them to come off of break."

Bud looked ill-at-ease again. He answered quickly. "They're pretty good, but they just went on a break, so it may be awhile." He hoped that she would get discouraged and leave sooner rather than later.

"Well, maybe I'll get on home then. But since I'm here, I'd like to take some pictures of this old place before I go. I used to come here in my twenties, and it brings back memories. Do you think you can help me out so I can get a move on?" she asked.

"Help you out?" he asked.

She had her phone out and took some pictures of the bar then turned to him, "Just take a quick selfie with me and that should do it. Then I can get on the road."

He agreed. Anything to get her on her way.

So she held her phone at arm's length and scooted up close to him. It was a little closer than he liked, but he held still to get it over with. She was saying something to him, but he could not quite understand her over the loud music.

"Sorry," she shouted. "It's so damned loud in here it hard to hear anything. Come a little closer."

When he leaned closer to her, she reached up and quickly planted a big kiss on his surprised lips, her camera flashing. He jerked away, shocked.

"That should do it," she said, suddenly all business-like. She shouldered her purse and walked away, calling over her shoulder, "Thanks, Bud." She looked at her phone as she walked, unworried about what her husband would say. He was never on social media, he didn't even have any accounts.

Within fifteen minutes, several versions of that kiss were posted on Facebook and Instagram with the caption, "Old Friends—now New Friends #hunky #thankslola."

CHAPTER 27

Dawn was still reeling from her Facebook fiasco and now had to deal with Rocky Breaux on a much bigger level. She had wanted to get back at Rocky for his insults at the cooking school, but she really did not want to go through with the gumbo competition. *"What a pain!"* she thought. She got Bea, then Trinity, on the phone for advice.

First Bea said, "You just need to apologize to Rocky, dear. Then it will all be over with. And don't feel bad about it. Everyone does something foolish now and then—especially on social media."

"Have you?" Dawn asked her friend hopefully.

"Well, no, not me, but you know—everyone else," she laughed. "So, just tell him you'd had a hard day and posted it in haste."

"You think so?"

"No, I don't think so," said Trinity when Dawn told her Bea's advice. "It won't work. I know Rocky, and I know you, and y'all are two of the stubbornest mules on planet Earth."

"Look who's talking!" said Dawn. "Once when were a kid, I told you not to play with your food. You were dunking toy soldiers in your oatmeal, for heaven's sake. And, of course, since I said something about it, you wouldn't eat oatmeal for a year without a toy soldier stuck in it!"

"I did like a breakfast that made you want to march into the new day." laughed Trinity.

"Ha-ha," muttered Dawn. "And Rocky was just as bad. You both drove me crazy."

When they got off the phone, Dawn decided to bite the bullet and take Bea's advice. She dialed Rocky's number.

He answered gaily, "I don't believe it! Is this The Bad Ass of Breaux Bridge?"

"Dammit, Rocky, you don't know when to quit, do you?"

"Mostly not," he said. "Wait, don't tell me. You're calling to apologize and admit that my cooking is amazing. Not only can I cook, but my mom's gumbo recipe is going to knock you senseless— because it's just truly the best. You'll feel like you never had gumbo before. And, of course, you want to apologize for being a smart-ass on social media about me."

Dawn felt her blood pressure building up dangerously and said, "Trinity said this wouldn't work, and she was right. I've never eaten your gumbo, Rocky, but if you made it, it's probably undernourished, cowardly, and should go back to the wrong side of the tracks again. Oh, wait—now I'm back to talking about you!"

"Oh my gravy - you're so funny, chérie. But your words are going to make it that much sweeter when I win our little challenge. You're not trying to back out, are you?"

"Wouldn't dream of it," said Dawn through clenched teeth. She took it one step further and solidified the whole mess, "My friend Helen is having a workshop at the Gumbeaux Sistahs Gallery coming up soon. I'll text you the date. We'll do the cook-off at noon and feed everyone at the workshop. Bring your pot of gumbo and your big mouth, and we'll settle this once and for all." She hung up before he could answer. Then she swore and kicked herself for her rotten temper.

CHAPTER 28

The next morning brought new challenges for Judith in the form of more Sistah meddling.

Since Bitsy had set up her dating site accounts for her, she knew all Judith's passwords. In the spirit of helping out — or, perhaps, forcing an issue — she'd logged in to one of the sites late the night before and set up a breakfast date for Judith without telling her about it till first thing in the morning. Judith had thrown up her hands in disgust when she'd found out about it. But then she's said to herself, laughing, "Oh, why not? Besides, this is what I get for getting the Sistahs involved!"

So later that morning, Judith entered through the double glass doors of the Abita Roasting Company café. She glanced around the room quickly, looking for the face that matched the one on her phone. She found it on a man waving to her from a corner table.

"Oh, whew!" she thought, *"I didn't get stood up this time at least. OK, let's just see what happens here. Please just let him be a normal human being."*

"Brian?" she asked, walking up to the table.

"Judith?" he answered with a smile. She offered her hand, and he took it warmly. "Thanks for coming out. I've been looking forward to our breakfast. Here, have a seat. Have you eaten here before?"

"OK," she thought. *"He seems nice, and he has warm hands and good manners. So far, so good."* She smiled back at him and told him that she had and that she was looking forward to getting to know him over coffee.

The waitress walked up as he asked Judith what she liked for breakfast. But before she could answer, he caught the waitress' eye, pointed to the menu and said, "We'll have two orders of the Cajun Praline Chicken and Waffles—and two coffees."

He folded up his menu again and handed it back to the waitress with a big grin directed towards Judith as if he were waiting for an "atta boy" from her. "Can't beat chicken and waffles!" he said.

Judith paused because she was actually stunned. She noticed that the waitress would not meet her eyes as she waited to see what Judith would say. Judith decided to be cool and folded up her menu too. True, she felt as if she had just folded up a tiny bit of her soul by not speaking up about his ordering for her like she was a child. "*OK,*" she told herself, "*Calm down,*" although she knew a red flag when she saw one. "*I actually like chicken and waffles anyway.*"

"That's fine," she told the waitress and turned back to Brian and asked, "So where are you from Brian?"

"I'm originally from Baton Rouge but went to school at Tulane and ended up staying in New Orleans after graduation." He went on to tell her how he had opened his law practice there years ago. Then how he had gotten married, had two children, and what each of them did for a living. He then walked her through his divorce in detail.

The waitress arrived with their food and he continued through mouthfuls. Judith nodded and smiled at him politely, but grew more anxious as the meal went on.

Finally, he paused, looked at her as if he suddenly realized she was there and asked, "Didn't you tell me you lived in the Lakeview section of New Orleans?"

"*Finally,*" she thought, and started to say, "Yes, I lived there for—"

He interrupted jovially, "I thought so. It's a great part of town—love the houses there. The ex-wife and I thought about living there at one time."

Judith's window of conversation opportunity was apparently over. Not his though. He told her how many dates he had been on through the app they had both used and how each of those dates had gone. He explained how he had adopted a greyhound named Ivan. He boasted that he owned a boat and docked it in Madisonville. He described his trip to Italy last summer in great detail.

Judith wasn't sure if he was a trial attorney or not, but could see how he might never have lost a case. He could probably talk his opponents, and possibly a whole jury, to death in the courtroom. Judith's whole body was numb from listening. The one thing the conversation never hit on at all—was Judith. Not that she was so eager to talk about herself, but his lack of interest in any detail about her was a bit shocking. He did not ask her any more questions all through the meal.

Aside from polite quips and agreeable expressions, Judith could have easily counted the number of words she had managed to contribute the entire date on one hand. She would have bet money that if Brian suddenly had to pick her voice out in some sort of lineup, he would never be able to in a million years.

He even told her when it was time to leave, which he did suddenly, and that he would walk her to the parking lot.

He opened her door her door and the last thing he said as she got in the car was, "Well, that was really fun. I think we'll do this again." Of course he had a good time. He loved nothing better than the sound of his own voice. He said, "Let's have dinner on Tuesday."

At last a chance to speak. She started the car and smiled at him as she drove away, saying, "I'll definitely have to let you know about that, Brian. The jury is still out." Brian might have been a self-centered bore, but he was a smart man. He could figure out what that meant.

CHAPTER 29

Judith was hanging a painting in the Gumbeaux Sistahs' Gallery when Dawn stormed in the front door.

"There's no way around it. I'm going to have to kill Rocky Breaux!" she hollered. "He's forced me into this gumbo competition thing now. I don't have time for this nonsense!"

Judith shook her head with sympathy, but said firmly, "Are you sure you didn't start all this yourself? Or at least prolong it?"

"Hey, you're supposed to be on my side!" fumed Dawn. She looked closely at her partner's face and pulled up sharply, "Wait. What wrong?"

"Oh, it's nothing," said Judith glumly, "Just a couple of little things—mostly it's about Lucy."

"Who's Lucy?" asked Dawn, at a loss. "A customer? Did someone ask you to paint something to match their couch again?"

"No, Lucy's the dog. You know, the pug," said Judith.

"You still have her? Wait—you named her?"

"Yes, well, I can't seem to find her owner. I've put up signs, placed her picture on online missing-dog sites, and contacted the pound and told them I found a pug, in case anyone had lost one. I even took her to a vet to see if she was micro-chipped, but no such luck. The vet looked her over and said that she was healthy, but it looked like she had been on her own for a bit. She was a bit on the scrawny side and full of fleas. So I had her treated for the fleas, and she's making up for the skinniness in spades. Man, that dog can eat!"

"So can I," grinned Dawn. "No fleas on me so far, though."

"That's not what I heard," said Lola, coming in the front doorway grinning. She was dressed for landscaping work. "Did I hear you say that you have a dog, Judith?" She walked over and helped herself to coffee.

Judith told her about finding the little pug. "The vet says she's about a year old, so she's still really just a pup, or a young teenager. I think she's a teenager who must have fallen in with the wrong crowd though. I've never seen such a bad little thing!""

"What does she do? And by the way, why are wearing those knee-high boots? It's kind of warm out today for that, isn't it?" Lola pointed to Judith's shoes and she and Dawn looked at her legs confused.

"I didn't want to wear these, but I had to!" said Judith, disgustedly. "It's definitely too warm for them, but Lucy keeps biting my heels! I can't walk anywhere in the house without her chasing me and gnawing on me like I'm an old bone. I know I'm getting up there in years, but c'mon—it's a little insulting!"

Dawn noticed that Judith was half-smiling as she complained. "Wait a minute—you like that crazy mutt! Maybe you've got yourself a dog after all. Am I right?"

"Oh no," said Judith emphatically. "When I get a dog, it's going to be a big, old, noble lab who will adore me, and protect the house, and people will want to make movies about it. And his name will be Blue."

"Sure, sure," grinned Dawn. "So why did you name her then? And why not just take over to the Humane Society? And why 'Lucy,' by the way?"

"Oh, I couldn't turn that little monster in. I know that the Humane Society takes great care of their animals, but how would we know who adopted her? They are a great no-kill shelter, and I send donations to help support them, but who knows who she would end up with? Even if they screen, and they do, seriously, how well can they know the new owners?"

"And the name—Lucy?" reminded Dawn.

"Oh well, I was thinking of the old *I Love Lucy* TV show and how that crazy redhead was always in trouble. Remember how her husband, Ricky Ricardo, would always be astounded by the problems she could cause he and would say in his Cuban accent, 'Lucy, 'splain!' I find it makes me want to kill her a little less if I yell, 'Lucy, splain!' when she is biting my feet."

"So you've taken to wearing high boots in hot weather and developed a Cuban accent," laughed Lola. "This dog better find its owner soon, or there's no telling what you'll be doing next. Maybe start doing paintings about a little blue dog!"

"The owner will show up soon," said Judith firmly. "What about your dog, Dawn? I thought you were gonna go pick one out."

"I think I'll just wait and see what happens at your house first," smirked Dawn.

"That's so kind of you," said Lola, rolling her eyes.

"Wait a second," said Dawn. "Didn't you say that there were a couple of things bothering you? What's the second one?"

Lola settled comfortably in a chair, "Yes, spill it, Judith. We're here to help."

"It's just that this dating thing has not been going very well. I'm trying, I really am. I've had a couple of dates now. The first was a no-show, and the second was boring and self-centered. And, you know, this is all your fault for getting me into this nonsense and getting me on those dating sites. I had no idea how awful they can be!"

"They work for many people though. You hear about it all the time," said Dawn.

"I've been on them," said Lola.

"No surprise there," said Dawn, grinning.

"She's right, Dawn. They can be really strange. But, yes, there are lots of people who make them work."

"Did they ever work for you?" asked Judith.

"I've met a few nice guys that way, but nothing that stuck. But I know what you mean about the awful part," Lola said, nodding.

"Right? If the sites aren't confusing because there are so many men to talk to all at once, then they are unbearable because of the crazies that show up. The things they say! Unbelievable!"

"Like what?" asked Dawn. "I've been married since Noah filled up his arc, so I wouldn't know."

"Oh, I haven't even been on that long, and I could tell you stories." said Judith, disgustedly.

"Wait," said Lola, chuckling, "Have you had a guy message you yet to ask if you were interested in a threesome because his wife was cool with it?"

Dawn's jaw dropped, "No way!"

"Oh yeah," said Judith, nodding. "And then there's the guy who said 'Hello Beautiful' in one message, and just because I didn't answer him within a few minutes, he messaged again and said, 'Never mind. Didn't realize you were such a snob—and probably ugly too!"

"Shut up!" said Lola, laughing.

"It's the truth," said Judith, smiling now.

"I remember this one guy messaged me and told me I was too old for him. And I hadn't even messaged him first. He just said that out of the blue. And, guess what, he was older than I was!"

"And there's more than one whose profile says things like 'No smokers and No fatties!' Charming, right? I'd marry him in a minute."

The sistahs were holding their sides laughing at this point.

Catching her breath, Judith said, "I have to say, this really isn't a lot of fun, but it's a fascinating slice of our culture—one I'd rather skip."

"Well, promise you won't give up yet," pleaded Dawn. "It hasn't been very long, and you know what they say—you're still in that 'Kissing the Frogs' stage."

"We'll see, Dawn. This pond looks like nothing but frogs, if you ask me."

"Lucy, 'splain!"
- Judith

CHAPTER 30

Trinity sat in Dawn's kitchen eating the gumbo Dawn had made the night before.

"Amazing as ever," said Trinity, scraping the last bit out of her bowl.

"As good as Rocky's?"

"Hard to say," said Trinity, musing. "It's been a while now since our cooking class. I remember his was very good though. It will be a close contest for sure."

"There's only one thing to do then. We've got to get ahold of some of his gumbo again to compare the two. I'm not sure how we'll do that though. Let me think a minute." She got quiet and tried to think as she idly let her fingers scroll through her Facebook feed. Meanwhile Trinity was reading the latest issue of Inside Northside magazine.

Suddenly, Dawn made a half-squeal, half-choking sound, startling her sister. She had swallowed down the wrong pipe, and Trinity started pounding on Dawn's back. But instead of holding her hand to her throat in the universal sign of choking, Dawn pointed to the computer and turned Trinity towards it so she could see.

Lillian Deslattes' Facebook page was up on the screen. The latest post showed Lillian and Bud out at night somewhere—together. It looked like a bar. And they were kissing.

Trinity screamed, "What the . . . !"

Catching her breath, Dawn, now white as a sheet, screamed, "C'mon Trinity, there's no time to waste!" She jumped up and grabbed her purse off of the counter.

At that same moment, Bud was on the phone with Lola, "You saw what Lillian posted; I know you did. You know it didn't mean anything, right? She tricked me into that kiss."

"I figured as much," said Lola disgustedly. "I felt sorry for you, actually."

Bud was quiet for a moment. Then he said, "Lola, it doesn't have to be this way. I miss you. Surely we can work things out differently."

"Bud, as far as I'm concerned, this just makes it all that much clearer how this should go down. You're gonna have to accept it. Look, I gotta go, there's someone at the door." She hung up and opened the front door.

"You're kidding me, right?" yelled Dawn. "Did you see what she posted?" Trinity and Dawn swept past Lola into her living room.

"Yeah, I saw it."

"So Lillian is dead now, right?" demanded Dawn, and Trinity nodded in solidarity. "Please tell me you put a hit on her because, if not, I know two sisters who are up for the job!"

"Nobody's killing anyone," said Lola, then added pointing to Dawn. "Unless you want to count the heart attack you're giving me over how crazy you are."

"Oh, you haven't seen crazy yet," said Dawn, her eyes wild.

"Well, actually I have," grinned Lola. "And on a daily basis!"

"So what are you going to do?" demanded Dawn.

"Dawn, I want you to listen carefully to me, OK?" Lola searched her friend's face for signs of understanding, "I'm not going to do anything."

"What? No, I won't let you do nothing. You have to at least hold her down and give her a crew cut. Or maybe we will just fill her car to the brim with pine straw mixed with honey. That would make one heck of a mess, wouldn't it?" Dawn had a maniacal look in her eyes.

"OK, let me try this again. Look, we all know Lillian. She obviously did this because she's still pissed at me for—well, you know—with her husband. It was such a stupid thing to do. But let's give this a pass, OK? She kind of owed me one."

"But, what about Bud?"

"We broke up, remember? If he wants to have a fling with Lillian, he can. He can do whatever he wants. He's a free agent now."

Dawn was stunned. "You're not mad? Hurt? Suicidal?"

"It doesn't feel great, but really there's nothing to be done."

Dawn was silent for a moment, and Trinity watched her big sister process the situation. Suddenly, Dawn got up and grabbed Trinity. "OK, Lola, if that's what you want. C'mon, Trinity, we've got shopping to do."

"OK," said Lola, as they hurried out the front door, "So you're not going to do anything stupid, right?"

"Oh, please. I most certainly am not. See ya later!" said Dawn, and waved goodbye.

Lola closed the door and heaved a sigh of relief.

Dawn hurried her sister to the car saying, "What we're gonna do is far from stupid!"

CHAPTER 31

Bea and Father Jim strolled around the grounds of the Grace Episcopal Church. "So, you've looked over all the information on the Lay Ministry Program, and it looks like you've made a decision about the classes, am I right?" said the kindly-faced priest.

"Yes, dear, I have."

"Well, good. It must be a relief to you. I know it was not an easy decision. It takes fifty hours of training, or about six months, and then you are allowed to help with some minor ministry work such as hospital and home visits. Not all churches offer this, and some have a completely different type of program—less formal—but we started our program some years back and feel it has been highly successful. "

"I'm excited to start," said Bea, nodding firmly.

Father Jim went on, "And, after all, you already have a ministry of sorts with your Friendship Bench. That must be very time consuming. It's astonishing really, what you and your friend Helen have done. Seriously, I wish I had thought of it," he chuckled.

"Well, you'll still have to interview with The Right Reverend Corbyn about all this. He's firm, but fair, and I'm quite fond of him. But you do have to clear it with him. Meanwhile, you're not going to be a Maria, are you?

Bea looked at him confused, "What's a Maria?"

"You know, there's one in every class. It's from the Sound of Music. Remember when all the nuns at the convent in the movie were walking around singing about the one trouble-making sister— 'How do you solve a problem like Maria?'"

"Oh!" laughed Bea, "No, they won't even notice me. I won't be any trouble at all."

He smirked at her, "Somehow, I'm just not believing that."

Bea stopped suddenly, and then grinned slyly at him. She pointed past him and said, "Take a look."

"What? What is it?" he asked, turning.

"What do you see under that tree over there?"

"It's a bench, I guess," he answered, puzzled.

"Yep, that bench right there is what gave me the idea to contact the church. I was walking past here recently and saw it —just sitting there, with nobody using it. What a waste!" she twinkled.

"Bea, are you thinking of expanding your operation onto church grounds?"

"Who me?" She laughed and replied, "Like I said, you won't even know I'm here." She winked at him. "But on the other hand — why not? Besides, you just said it was a good idea and that you wish you had thought of it—so I'll just tell the Bishop that you did. I'll bet churches have a lot of benches they're not using."

"Lord," he said, putting his hands together in prayer, "Save me—she's Maria-ing me already."

"You're not going to be a Maria, are you?"

- Father Jim Jacobs

CHAPTER 32

The following afternoon, Martin LeBlanc strolled down Columbia Street. He lived in Baton Rouge, and he did not get over to Covington very often except for the rare visit to see his sister in town. She usually went to visit him, but this was a special occasion. He was in town this week looking at property and thinking of moving closer to her. He had retired, and she was his only sibling.

His wife of thirty-three years had died a few years ago, and he had retired from his own architectural firm since then. Retirement left him looking around for a new beginning. His idea was to hit town, stay for a little while, and get the feel of Covington to see where he would like to buy or build.

He had never visited his sister's place of business before, and that was where he was heading now, hoping to take her to lunch at Toad Hollow Café. It was a cute, little place he's found with an interesting selection, including some healthy choices. His visit was a surprise, as he had just decided a couple of days ago to get in the car and take the drive. He parked downtown and thought he would walk for a few blocks and see what other businesses were around before stopping in to see her.

One business in particular caught his eye—the Gumbeaux Sistahs Gallery. He especially liked the name. Peaking in the front window, he spotted a woman sitting at a table playing the ukulele with her back to him. She had blondish hair and was wearing a long, flowing skirt. When she turned towards him for a moment, he was startled with sudden recognition.

"Isn't that the same crazy woman that I ran into in the cheese department at that little grocery?" he thought, squinting to make sure. He pushed closer to the glass. *"That's her, alright!"* He smiled, remembering how funny that little incident had been. She had been so embarrassed and quirky. He had thought about her several times since then, usually with a chuckle.

A mischievous glint came into his eyes and he thought he might have a little fun. Pulling open the door, he walked in.

"Hi," he said. "So, now you're the ukulele lady. I thought you were the cheese lady."

Judith turned around and looked at him in confusion. "I'm sorry?"

He pointed to her instrument, "Are you any gouda at that?" He grinned.

Realization dawned on her. She flushed to her roots. She still had not gotten over embarrassing herself that day.

"Oh, it's you!" she started. Then additional confusion clouded in, "How did you find me?"

His look was pure amusement at that moment. He had not exactly found her as much as he had stumbled onto her. "Honestly? Pure dumb luck," he said, his brown eyes twinkling.

Judith tamped down her embarrassment and straightened up. "Well, are you here to buy one of my paintings?" she asked. "Now that would be luck—but, not dumb, of course," She laughed nervously.

He looked around the gallery admiringly, "These are yours? They're wonderful!" He genuinely loved the colorful works.

"Yes, they're mine, and so is this gallery—along with my partner, Dawn Berard."

"Well, I'm impressed. I really am. I don't know whether to buy a painting, ask you for a ukulele lesson, or get some advice on cheese. You're a woman of many surprises."

"Oh, not so much," she laughed. "Just your normal, supernaturally talented goddess."

He chuckled at that and thought, *"And funny too. Also, easy on the eyes."*

"Are you full of surprises too?" she asked, surprised to find herself actually flirting. She thought, *"See! I knew I hadn't completely forgotten how. It's like riding a bike. Like jumping on my old Huffy!"*

He replied coyly, "Oh, I've been known to come up with one or two surprises in my time." He was grinning at her now. "How's this for a surprise—how would you feel about having dinner with me tonight?"

She blanched. "Oh! I didn't know you'd have *that* big a surprise! But, of course, I don't think I should go out with just anybody who walks through the door. All I know about you is that you like cheese."

"Martin Leblanc is the name. And you are . . . ?" He walked over to one of the paintings on the wall and read the signature, "Judith Lafferty? Wonderful Irish name!" He put out his hand to her.

"It's lovely to meet you, Martin," she shook his outstretched, warm hand.

"How about this, Judith Lafferty. I'm in town looking for a home to buy. Will you please meet me tonight at the Oxlot 9 restaurant a couple of blocks from here? It would help me a great deal in trying to figure out where to live. You probably know a lot about the area, right?"

She hesitated, searching his face for signs of affliction—flea, Ebola, or serial-killerness. Finding none, she took a bold step. "OK, Martin Leblanc, you have a . . . an appointment."

He grinned at her, liking what he saw. "You won't regret it, Judith. Now I'm going to walk away like Cool Hand Luke before I say something stupid and make you change your mind."

She laughed, "I've already beaten you to saying something stupid so, don't worry. It's your turn anyway."

"OK, I'll wait and say something stupid tonight. Count on it. And I'll count on seeing you. I'm glad we met again."

When he closed the door, Judith thought about calling the Sistahs right away, knowing that they would love to hear her report in about this latest romantic development. She could already hear Dawn saying, "This is it! It's the big one! Wear something sexy!"

But Judith decided that she would just keep this little furtherance to the cause to herself for now. She didn't want to jinx anything.

A big grin was spread across his face as he walked down the next block and entered the Covington Museum.

"Hello," he told the woman at the front desk. "Is Lillian Deslattes available?"

The woman dialed an extension, and in a moment, Lillian walked down the stairs. When she saw who was waiting for her, she exclaimed, "Marty! What is my big brother doing in town?"

"Are you any gouda at that?"
- Marty

CHAPTER 33

ucy was all decked-out in her new, pink harness and leash, and she was doing her best to yank Judith's arms out of their sockets as they walked down the street. At times, she would suddenly take off to the right, then change direction on a dime and take off to the left.

Judith's shoulder was on fire. "Good Lord, Lucy! We're taking a walk, not playing 'dislocate the human's shoulder!'"

They slowly continued in this way down the oak-lined street in Judith's neighborhood.

She noticed at one point that the pug's harness looked a little saggy, so she bent over to check on the snugness. Lucy grabbed this opportunity to jump up into Judith's face, startling her. The dog then pulled backwards from the leash as hard and as quickly as she could. To Judith's horror, the dog slipped from the harness and dashed off down the street. And just as suddenly, Lucy switched directions and ran full speed right at Judith.

"C'mon, Lucy! Come here! That's a good dog!" yelled Judith and held her arms out to the pup. Lucy tore right by her, passing her like the wind.

"Come back here, you crazy dog!" Judith felt panic rising and could easily imagine the worst-case scenario happening in the next few minutes. Lucy could get lost again—or worse, she could get hit by a car. She heard a rumbling and looked up the street just in time to see a car headed right for them. Lucy was circling Judith with a big doggy grin on her bad little face, having a grand-old time. Judith needed to act fact. She took off running up the driveway of the nearest house. Up for the chase, Lucy followed Judith, allowing the car to pass out in the street without incident.

But the car didn't go very far. In fact, it pulled into the driveway next door. A lady around Judith's age got out of her car and then bent over to reach back inside. Her arms came out holding a little rat terrier. Lucy took one look at the other dog and lost her mind.

The pug actually tried to climb up the front of the woman carrying her dog. The terrier practically screamed as he struggled with all its might to escape the woman and go after Lucy. The woman hollered and held on, all the while shooting dagger-laced looks at Judith.

"Oh my, I'm so sorry," said Judith, mortified. "My dog got out of her harness, and I just can't catch her. I hope she didn't hurt you!"

The woman did not say one word, but marched up her front porch steps, terrier still in her arms. She stood struggling with her keys to the front door.

Lucy never left the woman's side and continued to jump up on the woman's legs as the rat terrier barked like the world was ending.

Judith noticed that the porch was enclosed, except for the area by the steps. She made a decision and said loudly to the woman, "I'm sorry but I'm going to have to follow you up on your porch so I can trap my dog."

In a minute Lucy was cornered, and Judith held her by the scruff as she worked quickly to get the harness back on and adjusted. The woman, meanwhile, had gone in the house with a huff and slammed the front door.

Red-faced and embarrassed, Judith led Lucy away from the house and down the street, cutting their walk short and heading home. "Lucy, if I didn't like you, I swear I would kill you dead right now!" Lucy looked up at her name, grinned, wagged her rolled-up tail, and barked. Judith, still fuming, could not help but grin back at her.

"Lord," she thought, *"I don't know why you sent me this little, insane dog, but thank you for helping me get her back in her harness and not letting her get hurt!"*

She realized right at that moment how devastating it would have been if anything had happened to this little pug. Her heart hammered, and she felt tears in her eyes all the way home.

CHAPTER 34

Bea knocked on Helen's front door that afternoon. Helen opened it and scooted her friend inside. Together they set up the laptop computer on the dining room table, and Helen made coffee.

"He should be here any minute," said Helen. "I just want you here as a buffer between us. The boy is hard to get along with, and he is extra hard to reach. I would have met him at the gallery today, but Dawn and Judith closed early so that a plumber could get in and make some repairs."

"I'm happy to help, dear," said Bea. "Besides, I want to check on the young genius myself."

A few more minutes went by before the doorbell rang. When Helen let him into the house, he was dressed all in black, but this time he had added dark sunglasses to his look. "OK, let's get this over with," he said sourly, not removing his glasses.

Helen raised her eyebrows at Bea, who shook her head in response. Then Bea spoke up in a clear, strong voice, "Hello Cooper, it's good to see you again."

"Yeah," he grunted, while setting up his own laptop. He immediately launched into showing Helen the presentation he had created.

"Aren't you going to take off your sunglasses?" asked Helen, staring at him.

"Nah, I'm good," he said coldly. "Let's just get on with it."

He went through the slide show with Helen without saying a word but taking notes on the comments that Helen made. Bea added her opinion now and then too.

"What do you think of this part?" Helen asked him at one point.

"Doesn't matter what I think," he muttered angrily. "It never does. This is your deal, not mine."

Bea sat down close to him and whispered, "Do you remember what I told you about being rude to my friend? It's not going to happen, dear." She was looking at him with her eyes narrowed, and he started to look a little uncomfortable under her scrutiny. It was only then that Helen and Bea noticed the blue swelling around his left eye.

He suddenly jumped up and slammed shut his laptop case. "Look, I'm delivering what you asked me to, and now I have to go. I'll see you next week same time with the changes you want. That's what I'm paid for, not to be nice to you or your friend or anyone else."

He started to walk away, but Helen hurried to the front door to cut him off. "Listen, Cooper, your work is wonderful, and I'm very happy with it so far. But I just want to say something to you before you go."

"Don't bother," he said.

"I'm bothering," continued Helen. "Someone has hurt you. I can see your black eye." She took him by the arm. "Do you want to talk about it? Who did that to you?"

He pulled his arm away from her roughly. "Of course I don't want to talk about it. What could you possibly do? What can anyone do? Just forget about it, and let's get this stupid job done. I need the money."

He started out the door, but Helen called after him, "Cooper, just know that you can trust me if you need someone. You have my phone number, and you can call me anytime. Bea and I are good at helping people. I will help you if I can."

"Yeah right," he yelled back angrily, and lumbered up the street.

Helen turned back to Bea who said, "That's a hurting boy, Helen. He's not just going to show up on the Friendship Bench and talk. I'm not sure what anyone can do with a boy like that."

Helen was shaken and said, "I'm going to pray about it."

"I'm going to join you, my friend."

"Remember what I told you about being rude to my friend? It's not going to happen, dear."

- Bea

CHAPTER 35

The Right Reverend Corbyn stood up behind his desk to welcome Bea for their appointment at his office in his downtown New Orleans office. Bea looked around and immediately felt a certain serenity amidst the book-lined walls, the fine, old wooden desk, and heavy leather chairs. A simple, large, wooden cross hung behind the Bishop's chair—a reminder of why they were all there.

"Come in, come in, and sit down, Ms. Walker," he said, as he shook hands with the diminutive woman in her sixties with the piercing blue eyes. He, himself, was a tall, graying giant of a man with the kindest face Bea had seen in a long time.

They chatted a few minutes over tea about where they each grew up. She was from New Orleans, and he was originally from Philadelphia and happy to be living in New Orleans for the past ten years. He was affable, and Bea relaxed while sizing him up and getting ready for his real questions.

She already liked him, and then he jumped right into business, and she liked him even more.

"So, we're here to talk about your entry into the Lay Ministry Program at Grace. It's a big commitment, Bea. Are you up for the time it takes to complete the program? It starts in a few weeks, and it will take up six months of your life."

"I've got plenty of time."

He laughed, which make his soft brown eyes crinkle deeply at the corners. "You know, Ms. Walker, Reverend Jim says you're trouble, but that he loves you."

"Please call me Bea—and the feeling is pretty much mutual," said Bea with a quiet smile.

He appraised the small woman across from him with her wrinkled, cherubic face. "I've never heard Reverend Jim speak so highly of a candidate for that program before. You've really impressed him. Or bewitched him—one of the two. But I have to admit that, seeing you today, you are not what I expected. I expected someone that was . . . um." He stalled, searching for the words.

"Taller?" she asked, laughing.

"Exactly," he said, relieved. "I appreciate your humor, Bea."

"Well there's nothing I can do about my—uh—height or anything else like that, Bishop Corbyn. I can only do something about my wish to help people, and I'm good at that. Now, I know that Father Jim told you about our little ministry that we call the Friendship Bench." The Bishop nodded, and she went on. "The reason I'm interested in the Lay Ministry is that I simply want to educate myself in order to help people further, both in their personal lives and in their spiritual quests. I only know where my quests guide me, and I want to be trained to meet the challenge. I'm already helping these people. I just want to help them more through more Friendship Benches. Your training will help me counsel our bench sitters as well as myself. Plus, I would so welcome the chance to help out in the congregation with whatever ministry duties I'm called to do for the church as well. So the question is, can you help me help these people?"

The Bishop was slightly taken aback, suddenly feeling as if he were the one being interviewed. He could read the passion and purpose in this woman, and found it inspiring. "That's what we're here to talk about," nodded the Bishop.

"Besides," Bea went on, "We humans always need to be finding ways to be closer to God, and this feels like it's calling me to come closer."

"I can't argue with that," he nodded solemnly.

Suddenly, she looked up at him with a grin. "Don't worry, Bishop, I won't try to take your job."

He gaped at her for a moment, then roared with laughter. "I'm going to like having you around, Bea."

"We humans always need to be finding ways to be closer to God."

- Bea

CHAPTER 36

The wind was picking up, getting ready for a storm. Even though the restaurant was only three blocks from her house, Judith drove. She did not want to arrive at the first decent date she had had in years looking like the wreck of the Hesperus.

She had dressed carefully in a black dress and a royal blue wrap with felted flowers embroidered onto it. A chain of silver and small silver earrings completed her outfit. She felt that she looked California Casual, as she called it—casual, yet chic.

She walked into Oxlot 9 and spotted Martin sitting at a table near the front windows. He wore nice jeans with a black shirt and sports coat. She definitely approved.

"You look beautiful. Elegant, even," he said, and she smiled.

"And you look rather handsome, Martin," she replied. While he seated her like a gentleman he said with a chuckle, "Please call me Marty. Martin is for people I don't know or don't want to know."

They ordered two glasses of pinot noir. "Are you a red wine person too?" she asked.

"Pretty much," he nodded. "It feels like the adult version of a glass of wine."

"Isn't that the truth?" she commented, adding with a laugh, "Don't tell my friends this, but I can order an expensive glass of white wine, and when it comes, I feel as if I'm still waiting for the real thing to arrive!"

They talked about their backgrounds. He told her he had been born in New Orleans and now lived in Baton Rouge. He was a widow and was looking to move back to this area where his sister lived. He touched for a minute on how his wife had died from breast cancer, and how it had been a tough few years.

She told him how she was also from New Orleans. They were both from the Lakeview area, as it turned out. He had gone to Cor Jesu, later Brother Martin, and she had gone to St. Joseph Academy and later on to the University of New Orleans. He went to LSU in Baton Rouge where he stayed after graduation to open his own architectural firm. She had traveled and lived around the country, settling down eleven years ago at one job in Covington. She told him how, a few months back, she and her partner Dawn had opened the gallery and how they had had so much trouble from one horrible, local woman that they had almost had to close it, but that they had overcome their problems and were now doing well. Her eyes lit up when she spoke about how the gallery was doing.

He watched her as she talked, unable to keep from looking at her animated expressions and pretty face, especially when she smiled.

They split a dozen oysters, and then dinner arrived. They never stopped talking and relaxed easily into each other's company.

For dessert, they split a cheesecake slice with raspberry sauce. Her first bite left a splotch of red sauce on the side of her mouth. He pointed to his mouth to let her know about it, and she reached for her napkin in her lap and found it gone.

"Oh good Lord," she said. "I'm always losing my napkin. I think there are leprechauns that lurk under tables trying to make people feel silly by stealing the napkins off their laps."

He teased her, "You had one job, Lafferty—you just had to look after your napkin while I fed you gorgeous food. Here, use mine, and I'll get you another one."

He reached for his napkin and found it gone too. He turned a little red at having to admit it, then laughed. "Oh man, I only had two jobs—get you a wonderful dinner and guard my napkin from the leprechauns!" They both started laughing and found they did not want to stop. It felt so good to laugh.

She finally managed to stop, holding her sides, and she suddenly told him, "Marty, I'm having a wonderful time."

His eyes caught hers and something clicked in that moment. They both knew it. She smiled shyly at him, and he gazed warmly into her pretty hazel eyes.

They talked about his move to Covington. Judith described her favorite neighborhoods, and he mentally took notes on where he wanted to visit with his realtor the next day. He told her that he was also keeping an eye out for one-bedroom apartments for his grand-niece, Nancy, who was thinking of moving here too. "I hope she does. She's a great kid. And then if I move here, I'll get to see my sister, my favorite grandniece, and maybe even you."

Later, when he walked her to her car, she hesitated for a moment, telling herself that she was unsure of what to do, or of even what she wanted to do. In actuality, she knew that what she wanted was to kiss him goodnight. It had been a very long time since she had been kissed by someone that was truly kissable.

He moved closer to her. She was not disappointed.

CHAPTER 37

The next morning, Marty LeBlanc left his room at the Southern Hotel and walked up to Columbia Street, looking for a coffee shop. As a retired architect, he admired some of the buildings on the street and was especially taken with the unique Brunner Gallery Building with its unusual metal flourishes over the doorway and in the building corners.

The design made him smile, and he was already smiling inside. *"Yes, Covington is looking more and more like it might be a good move for me,"* he thought.

He knew that it would be somewhat painful for him to leave his long-time Baton Rouge home. His wife Elaine and he had lived there since he had started his own firm, LeBlanc Architects, many years ago. Marty had studied at LSU and met Elaine there, who was getting her degree in education. Elaine came from a big Baton Rouge family, so after college, instead of returning to his hometown of New Orleans, Marty stayed and opened his business there. They had one daughter when they were both in their thirties, and she was the pride of their lives. She lived in California now, and they had weekly phone calls and yearly visits to keep close. Then Elaine had died of that horror - cancer. Watching his adored wife wither away from the monstrous disease was the hardest thing Marty had ever done. He took some time off of work in order to take care of her during her last year. He could have gone back at that point, but he decided that enough was enough and retired shortly afterward.

The trouble was that Marty was lonely. He and Elaine had been socially active, and his business had kept him hopping. It had taken him a few years since her death, but Marty was ready for something new in his life. He had tried hobbies—cooking, gardening, reading, even some watercolors, but it did not feel like enough, somehow.

He had always been fairly close with his sister, Lillian. She had lived in Covington with her husband and grown children since their old college days, and he had visited a few times over the years. He had even played a round or two of golf with Lillian's husband Jack, but he was not the fanatic that Jack was. Still, they got along just fine, and Marty had always enjoyed the visits. Recently it had entered Marty's mind that he needed to change more than his list of hobbies. A clean-sweep was what he had in mind—selling the old place and starting over. So this weekend was his first foray into actually putting those pieces in motion. He had called a realtor, packed a bag, and headed out for a new adventure.

He ordered a latte at St. John's Coffeehouse, sat outside on the mesh-metal chairs, and called Lillian.

"Hello, you! What are you up to?" said Lillian into her phone.

"I'm still in town, and I've been running around talking to a realtor and getting a feel for the place."

"Sounds serious, Marty. So you are definitely thinking of moving here? That would be wonderful to have my favorite brother nearby."

"Not to mention, your only brother," he chided playfully.

"Well, yeah, that too," Lillian laughed.

"So, yes. I'm thinking seriously about it, and oddly enough, I may have an additional incentive at this point to make the move."

"Really? Tell me about it."

He smiled as if he could not quite believe what he was about to say. "Let's just say that my incentive is of the female persuasion."

Lillian was quiet for a moment. She felt shocked and happy all at the same time, as this was the first time she had heard her brother talk about a woman since his wife passed. "Oh Marty, is that true? I'm so happy for you! When can I meet her?"

"Well, it's early days yet, Lillian. She and I are still in the courting stage, shall we say. But I'll admit, I like her. I've had a wonderful time with her."

Lillian laughed. "Only you would say 'courting.' And I have to admit, I like hearing it. So who is this mystery woman?"
"Something tells me I should just keep her a mystery for a little while longer. I hope you don't mind. I'm just not even sure she's real yet myself. I just don't want to jinx it."

"OK, OK. But you can expect me to ask you at least once an hour until you give up a name," she said, laughing.

"If you didn't, I would know you weren't my sister, but some alien who is actually good at secrets."

"Ha!" she laughed loudly. "OK, I'm crossing my fingers for your happiness—no matter what."

"Thanks, Lillian, I could use it." He hung up and thought about his date last night with Judith. He could not get her off his mind. He grinned and whispered out to the universe, "Thank you."

CHAPTER 38

The next morning, Dawn met Trinity at Café du Monde in the French Quarter, where they did not even consider counting calories and splitting an order of beignets. They each got a full order and delighted in every hot, doughy, sweet bite.

They talked things over while they finished their breakfast. Trinity said, "This is a good plan, Dawn. If it works, we'll be able to taste and analyze his cooking, and make sure you can beat him."

At that moment, Trinity's friend Natalie walked up and joined them. She was wearing worn jeans, old sandals, and a scarf around her head like a gypsy. It reminded Dawn that before Trinity married Harry, opened her own gallery, and became a walking, talking socialite, she had been a starving artist in the French Quarter who had had some interesting but, at times, questionable friends.

"You made it!" Trinity shouted happily. "Natalie, this is my sister, Dawn."

"Dawlin', it's a pleasure," said Natalie, taking Dawn's hand.

"Hi, Natalie. Please join us. Now, how do you two know each other?" asked Dawn.

"My girl Trinity and I used to hang out in Jackson Square together. She was selling paintings, and I did these shotgun-house sculptures. I live in St. Bernard, and my brother, Erroll, always drove me in early Saturday mornings. I always saved us both our usual selling spots along the Jackson Square fence. Those were the good old days. And we've stayed in touch."

"I still carry a few of Natalie's pieces in the gallery. Gotta support our local artists," said Trinity. "And our friends too, of course."

"It's hard to make a living as an artist, so I'm glad you thought of me for this little job." Natalie smiled slyly. "So, who are we gonna rob?"

Dawn choked on her coffee. Trinity laughed loudly. "Natalie is just kidding, sister. She has a wicked sense of humor."

"Uh, sure, I knew that," said Dawn, blushing.

Natalie and Trinity grinned at each other, enjoying their little joke. Trinity reached into her purse and brought out a small mason jar and handed it to Natalie. "OK, put this in your purse. You're going to need it. This should be a pretty fun job, Natalie. We've already bought you a ticket to get in. All you have to do is sit in the cooking class. They'll serve you lunch there. And when the instructor, Rocky Breaux, is not paying attention, get yourself up to the stove and fill up this jar with his gumbo. We don't need any rice, just the gumbo."

"Wait, so the job comes with lunch?"

"Yep," answered Dawn.

"Sweet!" said Natalie. "I'm starved. This should be a piece of cake."

"OK, your class is at eleven, so afterwards, meet us across the street from the school, and we'll pay you and take the gumbo. Got it?"

"I'd better get a move on then, dawlin'. It's almost eleven. But why are you stealing gumbo, Trinity? I know you can afford to buy some. And why don't you just go to the class yourself?"

"We can't," answered Dawn. "The instructor is my enemy. So this is a kind of spy mission."

"Got it," said Natalie, nodding. "That makes it even sweeter. Are you sure there's nobody we can rob while you're here?" She elbowed Trinity and winked.

"I'll give it some thought while you're eating that trashy gumbo," said Dawn drolly.

An hour later, Dawn and Trinity stood outside and across the street from the New Orleans School of Cooking. They kept an eye on the front door of the shop, waiting for Natalie to get out of class and deliver the goods.

The school doors opened, and a small crowd walked out, obviously a class letting out. Natalie was in the middle of the group.

Dawn's eagle-eyes honed in on Natalie. "Oh no, she's empty-handed!" she groaned.

Trinity started to say something when she and Dawn both realized that Rocky Breaux was walking across the street towards them right behind Natalie.

"Oh my gravy!" he said disgustedly when he reached them. Natalie stood next to him, looking sheepish.

"Dawn Berard, if you're going to spy on my gumbo, be smart enough to not hang around right across the street. You could have stood on the corner or around the block. Don't you know I could spot you anywhere from two blocks away? Seriously, do you think I never get out of the kitchen?"

Natalie mouthed, "Sorry" to Dawn.

Trinity spoke up, "Aw Rocky, I'm sorry, but you know how competitive Dawn is. It seemed like a fun adventure to me. And I thought we could have had a good laugh over this after you two battle it out."

"We still will, Trinity girl," grinned Rocky. "But when that time comes, we'll be laughing because I will have beaten her at her own game." He turned to walk back to the shop and yelled over his shoulder, "For gravy's sake, you two, stay out of trouble—and stay out of my kitchen!"

The three women walked slowly up the street not speaking. When they got to the corner, Natalie stopped and fished inside her purse. Then, miraculously, she pulled out the Mason jar filled with beautiful, brown gumbo.

Trinity gasped, and Dawn hooted with laughter, "How did you do it?"

Natalie grinned. "He actually saw me standing near the pot so I thought it was all over with, but then he spotted you both through the front windows. While he spied on you two, I filled the jar and stuck it in my purse."

"Natalie!" said Trinity. "If I ever do a bank heist, you're going to be the first person I call!" She laughed and hugged her old friend.

Natalie said seriously, "If you ever rob a bank, Trinity, I'll be the first to sign up for the job."

Dawn laughed giddily.

"No. Seriously," said Natalie, not smiling now.

Dawn smirked as she paid Trinity's friend with an envelope of cash and said, "Yeah, you two will make great cell mates." Then she reached for the full jar—which slipped from her hands and crashed in a sloppy mess on the sidewalk.

"Bud, my friends have a right to their own brand of craziness. Let's face it—we're all ridiculous. I just have to love them anyway"

- Lola

CHAPTER 39

Trinity drove while Dawn shouted, clenching her fists in rage. "Dammit! We were so close!"

They were on the I-10. Trinity took the Bonnabel exit and headed up Veterans Boulevard, looking for a place to eat lunch before heading back home.

"Look," said Trinity, her head swinging around, looking for oncoming traffic. "I think you're putting too much emphasis on tasting Rocky's gumbo. You need to back off and trust in our mom's gumbo. It was always amazing, and everyone said so."

"Do you really think so?" Dawn looked at her hopefully.

"I'm positive," nodded Trinity. "Have a little faith. Where is my confident, bad-ass, big sister?" Trinity grinned at her.

Dawn winced at the nickname although it did not really bother her when Trinity teased her about it—only when everyone else did.

"Yeah, just get over it and move on. I love Rocky, but this is mom's gumbo we're talking about. You'll win, hands down. So try to cool down before you have a stroke."

"OK, I will. It will take me a little while, but I'll get there." Then she suddenly shouted and pointed, "Trinity—Look there!"

"Well, I'll be darned," said Trinity.

"It's Broussard Nurseries—right there! Tell me this isn't fate! This is our next stop on today's list of missions. We can kill two birds with one stone on this trip. Pull in, and let's go have a little talk with Mr. Bud Broussard, shall we?"

They parked and headed into the front entrance which was lined with beautiful arrangements of plants, flowers, and garden décor. They walked up to the front counter and said, "We're here to see Bud Broussard."

The woman behind the counter pointed down an aisle of flora to an office building in the back. They made their way to the main office and found it empty except for a young woman working behind a computer. "We're looking for Bud," they told her.

"He's out with Scotty, our foreman. I think you'll find them in the side yard with the shrubs."

Bud and Scotty watched the two sisters advance. Scotty whispered, "Uh oh, they look mean. Should I call the cops?"

Bud sighed and closed his eyes for a moment. "No thanks, Scotty. I'll handle this. Would you please check on the fern delivery for me?"

"Sure thing, boss," said Scotty, moving off but keeping one eye on the two approaching, large, beautifully dressed, menacing women.

"Hello, Dawn. Trinity," said Bud warily.

"Don't talk," hissed Dawn. "You just listen." She was almost as tall as he was, and Bud was not convinced that he was not about to be clouted in the head.

"How dare you," she began. "Not only do you push away one of the best women on the planet, but you take up with one of the worst. Lillian Deslattes! Really, Bud? Are you freaking kidding me?"

Trinity narrowed her eyes to slits and sneered. "You sure as heck better be kidding!"

"Now, ladies . . . ." he began.

"No talking!" said Dawn and took a step forward menacingly. "I just came here to tell you that I don't know what it is with men your age. The older we all get, the more handsome you think you are. I'm here to tell you it's not true, dude. My girl Lola is twice too good for you! And Lillian Deslattes? Really? It's just beyond comprehension."

"Isn't it though?" asked Trinity incredulously. Then she scowled "How could you, Bud?"

"Our girl is hurting back home—and for what? She's worth two of you," said Dawn. "I hope I never see your face again. C'mon, Trinity, let's get out of this dump!"

They turned around and marched angrily between the rows of plants. Just as they rounded a corner, Dawn turned back to make sure Bud was watching, pointed at a nearby begonia, and then knocked it off the shelf to the concrete sidewalk.

Trinity giggled, "Dawn, you really are a badass!"

Scotty walked quickly up to Bud, "Those women are scary, boss. I hope they never come back."

Bud sighed and took out his phone.

Bud told Lola about his visit from the two sisters.

"Lola, you've got to get your friends under control. You and I have made our peace with our decision, but they obviously have not."

"Bud, my friends have a right to their own brand of craziness. Let's face it, we're all a little ridiculous. I just have to love them anyway. But sure, I see what you mean, and I'm sorry. I'll handle it," said Lola, rubbing her forehead anxiously.

"OK," he said. He hesitated. "Lola, are you sure you want things to be this way?"

"We've been all through this. It has to be this way."

He sighed again. He did a lot of that these days. "OK, you're right. But it doesn't mean I have to like it. Let me rephrase that. I don't like it. I miss you. Can't we please be together?"

"I'm sorry, Bud."

"Those women are scary. I hope they never come back."

- Scotty

CHAPTER 40

No one had responded to Judith's inquiries about the missing pug. "This is highly suspicious," she told the little dog, who was nibbling at her bare heels. "Could it be that your owners were trying to get rid of you? Maybe they moved to Madagascar, with no forwarding address, so you couldn't bite them anymore."

Judith's heels hurt from the pug chasing and nipping at her when she walked. She made sure she was fully clothed and had shoes on at all times. Her ribs hurt too because Lucy's favorite place to chase her tail and try and to catch it in her teeth was on Judith's lap. The day before, when Judith sat on the couch next to the pug, Lucy "accidentally" bit Judith instead of her tail.

"Lucy!" she yelped, "'Splain!"

Since Lucy had arrived, Judith had to vacuum several times a week, as the house constantly threatened to be covered in dog hair. The pug shed like it was sitting in a barber's chair.

"What if nobody claims you?" she asked the pug and sat down on the couch. "Am I supposed to keep you? You're so much trouble!" Then she added, after a moment's thought, "You know, when I dreamed of getting a dog, I had in mind a big, friendly, loyal mutt named Shep or Blue. I pictured him in a movie where we would be separated, and he would have to cross over mountains and at least one ocean on a quest to get back to me."

While Judith mused, Lucy chose that moment to put her paw on Judith's chest and look her right in the face, her big, brown, sad-looking pug eyes inches away from her. The little pug licked Judith on the cheek, wagged her tail, then curled up in Judith's lap and trustingly fell right to sleep. Judith petted the dog's little, velvet ears and smelled her warm, puppy, corn-chip fragrance, and felt her heart melt in her chest.

"Dammit," she said and shook her head with a tiny smile.

CHAPTER 41

The sistahs were eating gumbo in Dawn's kitchen a couple of days later.

"So, do we understand one other, Dawn? Bud and I are splitting amicably. What's happening between us is a joint decision. There's no blame to be had. And that means, there will be no more showing up at his business and giving him the business!"

"Yeah, well, it just doesn't feel right. Someone had to say something," pouted Dawn as she ladled up more bowls of brown, rich liquid.

"Someone did. Me. I did. Everything's been said that had to be said. Really. That deal at his business was going too far. You freakin' always go too far!"

"I was just trying to do the right thing. I'm sorry," Dawn mumbled. "I guess I was a bit of an idiot."

"Oh, you were the CEO of idiots this time."

"Well, he hurt my feelings too. I wanted so much for you to be happy together."

"It's not about you, Dawn. And if you must know, the split was my idea."

"What? But you love Bud!"

"Now, dear," interrupted Bea, "Lola knows her own heart."

"Yes, we have to support her," said Helen, "Not make it worse for her. She's obviously going through something. Let's help her get through it."

Judith added earnestly, "Lola, if you need us, please speak up."

"Don't worry. I will. I know I can count on you if I need you. And Dawn, I said *if* I need you, OK? And besides, you know you'd be the first one I'd call, right?"

"OK, I'll try," said Dawn. "But if you ever want to let loose the Kraken on that guy, let me know."

"OK," laughed Lola, then she remembered something, "Oh, speaking of letting loose, my parents are throwing their big, annual, blowout barbecue next month." She told them the date and time. "Can everyone come?"

Bitsy said, "I can't wait, Lola! And that ought to cheer us all up."

"I love your parents," said Dawn, excited. "And they give the best parties. What can we bring?" She was happy that the subject had changed from her transgression.

"Whatever you'd like. My parents are cooking steaks and burgers, and we've got the dessert covered. I spoke to Bitsy already and she is going to make her famous Praline Cake for my parents."

"Ooh, those are amazing! Ok, I'll make gumbo," said Bea. "And rice too, of course."

"And I'll make potato salad for the gumbo," said Dawn.

"I'm thinking homemade breads and rolls," said Judith. "And maybe a pot of baked beans?"

"It all sounds wonderful," said Lola happily. "There'll be other folks coming too. You know my parents—they'll invite everyone. And if they don't, my brothers will."

Judith thought Lola looked cheerier and hoped the barbecue would give her friend something to look forward to.

"OK, mark your calendars. It'll be a blast."

"Wouldn't miss it, dear," said Bea.

The women helped themselves to more of Dawn's gumbo.

"This is perfect, as ever," said Judith appreciatively.

"It really is exceptional," said Bea.

"Yes, it's amazing," agreed Lola, then added with a wink, "Almost as good as my mom's."

Dawn snorted at the sistahs' standing joke, then added, "Just as long as it's better than Rocky Breaux's."

"I think it's killer," said Helen. "So, are we all set for the cook-off at my workshop?"

"Yes. I'll be glad to get it over with and shut that Rocky Breaux's big mouth once and for all," said Dawn hotly.

"Good," thought Lola with a sigh. *"I hope the cookoff distracts her and keeps her from harassing Bud anymore."*

CHAPTER 42

Helen waited for Cooper at the gallery the next afternoon, but he was late. They were meeting to go over last minute changes to Helen's workshop slide show.

Judith was behind the register. She asked, "Is he always late?"

"No. Well, no more than a few minutes anyway."

"Is this him?" Judith asked as the front door opened, and the young man, laptop in hand, slouched through the door, wearing his usual, dark NO t-shirt, unwashed jeans, and dark glasses. He plunked down into the chair next to Helen and said, "OK, tell me what you need."

Helen looked at him, ignoring his normal rudeness, sensing that he was even more agitated and gloomier than usual. "Hi, Cooper," she said carefully. "I'm glad to see you."

"But you're very late," hollered Judith from behind the counter, thinking, *"Helen is way too nice for her own good sometimes. This guy needs to be called on his rudeness."*

"Cooper, this is my friend and co-owner of this gallery, Judith Lafferty. Judith, meet Cooper Landry."

"Hey there Cooper," said Judith with a tentative smile. He grunted a return greeting.

Then he and Helen went over the work and cleaned up the presentation, bringing it to a state that made Helen happy and confident about her workshop.

Cooper, once again, did not take off his sunglasses, and Helen, once again, just could not let it go. "Cooper, I can't help but notice you're wearing the glasses again. Is your eye still healing, or this a new injury?"

The young man got to his feet saying, "OK, I don't ask you personal questions, do I? So, you're sure as hell not going to ask me any either. None that I'll answer anyway." He started gathering his laptop up.

"Wait, Cooper, before you go. I know it's personal, but, well, look at me . . ."

He kept his face down but glanced up at her.

"I don't know what this is about, but I'm worried about you. If you need someone to talk to, please let me know. You can trust me, I promise."

"Yeah sure," he mumbled. "Look, I'm good. I'll see you at the workshop. Bring my money—cash. That's all you need to know about me."

"You have my number. Please call me if you need me."

He walked out the gallery front door without another word. Judith gaped after him, shaking her head while Helen just stared at the closed door, tears starting to form in her eyes.

CHAPTER 43

Lola stood in Judith's backyard with her hands on her hips. "Yep, you're right, Judith. It's not so much of a bog-garden as it's just—a bog," she laughed.

Judith smiled, "Well, that's why you're here. I suck at this. I don't know much about plants or gardening, and everything I plant disagrees with my decisions. The only thing I've had any luck with are the irises. So, I had this vision that a bed of them could run across the back yard behind the boardwalk, and the deep purple color would look like a running river. That's what it looks like in my head anyway. Of course, then I open my eyes, and I'm back to the bog."

Lola walked to the back steps. "It's a wonderful idea, really. And I can help you out with all of it. But I'm not sure why you think the irises are doing well. They look a bit run down to me. Almost like a baby elephant got loose in here and danced a jig."

Judith sighed, "Well, they were doing well, until . . ." At that moment, Lucy jauntily pranced up to the steps and laid yet another ripped-up iris bulb at Lola's feet.

"Here's the baby elephant now," scowled Judith.

"Oh no!" said Lola. "Can she be trained?"

"Who? The dog or the iris?" sighed Judith. "My money's on the iris."

CHAPTER 44

On Monday morning, Helen picked up the phone in her kitchen. She nervously made the call that she had been thinking about all weekend to the high school guidance counseling office.

"Hello, Miss Smith? Helen Hoffmann here. I'm the woman who hired Cooper Landry to help me with my workshop, remember?"

"Of course, Helen. How is everything working out? I've been meaning to check in with you."

"Well, Cooper is delivering on the work in every way. He's a very talented young man."

"That's great to hear. Is there something I can help you with today?"

"It's about Cooper," said Helen, pausing. "To tell you the truth, I'm very worried about him."

"Oh dear, is it his attitude? I know he can be a little trying . . . "

"No, not really. Although it's certainly part of his getup, isn't it?" Helen laughed a tiny bit, then said, "No, I'm wondering about the black eye he has. And it's not his first either."

"Oh no!" said Miss Smith. "Not again."

"Has this happened before?" asked Helen.

"I'm afraid so."

"Has he been fighting at school?"

"No, not that I'm aware of. Although, his attitude hasn't made him many friends around here. But I haven't heard of any fighting lately."

"Do you think it might be coming from his home situation then?"

"Listen, this is completely off the record, but I'm so worried about that boy. It certainly could be happening at home. Remember I mentioned when we first met that his home life is not ideal. He lives with his stepfather, who is unemployed. The police have been to his house a couple of times for alcohol-related incidents. I do what I can for the boy at school, but it's up to the police and Cooper himself to decide if he is in danger."

"Is there anything we can do? He's got a brute of a shiner. I'm not sure if he's getting any medical attention."

"Hi stepfather is too slippery, and Cooper always backs him up for some reason. But if we can get Cooper to admit that someone is abusing him in his home, then we may be able to help. It's all up to him."

CHAPTER 45

Trinity knocked on the door to Rocky Breaux's office at the cooking school. "Rocky, are you in?" she shouted.

She faintly heard him call out, "C'mon in." She opened the door and found him at his desk surrounded by a pile of food receipts and leaning into his computer screen.

"Oh my gravy, Trinity! I'm so glad to see you!" He jumped up and ran to hug his old friend.

"Rocky, I'm so glad to hear you say that."

"What's up, girl?" he asked, holding her at arm's length and peering into her worried eyes.

"Oh, you know, the gumbo competition between you and Dawn. I've been shoved right in the middle of it all, and I didn't want you to forget that you're my best bud, and I love you to pieces."

Tears immediately sprang into Rocky's eyes. "You don't know what it means to hear you say that. You've been in my heart since we were kids. An exploding pressure cooker couldn't blast you out. I was so afraid I'd lose you over this nonsense."

"Not a chance, Rock. But tell me, do you really have to go through with the competition? Can't we just call the whole thing off?"

"There once was a time I would have said 'yes,' but it's too late now. Social media has made certain that my reputation is at stake. I keep hoping Dawn will get tired of the whole thing and back out."

"Do you not know my sister at all?" They both laughed nervously.

"I guess it just got out of hand. I'm sorry, Trinity. I didn't mean to cause you any trouble."

"Don't worry about me, but you and Dawn love each other too. I don't want to lose you, and I sure don't want Dawn and you to lose each other either. Seriously—with our childhood? We've been through too much together."

"But what can I do? I can't back out. My whole company here is rooting for me and now the press is aware of it too. The posts on Instagram and Twitter are demanding that the cook-off happen. We're just going to have to bite the bullet and get it over with."

"I was afraid you'd say that. But in that case, Dawn wants me to be sure and tell you that the cook-off at Helen's workshop is a definite go. And I'm supposed to tell you the rules. So, here goes: the gumbo will be pre-made and reheated on site, and Dawn will supply the rice and drinks. The workshop attendees will be the judges, and it will be an anonymous judging. They won't know who cooked which gumbo. Dawn and Judith will call the local press in Covington and you can tell your press contacts in New Orleans. That way Helen's workshop will get free PR, the gallery will get mentioned, and so will the cooking school. We'll sell the gumbo for five dollars a cup to the public after the judges have been served, and proceeds will go to Safe House, the local shelter for women and children escaping domestic abuse. A representative of Safe House will be there too. So, what do you think?"

"Sounds good. There's some great ideas there, and everyone wins—especially me!" he laughed. "So, of course, I'll be there. It'll be easy for me. All I have to do is bring a big pot of gumbo. Actually, if you'll remember, my sister lives in Covington, and I may just go to her place the day before and do all the cooking there. That way, I won't have to go far with that big pot. So, yes. Tell Dawn it's definitely on. Meanwhile, do you think you can get her to calm down a little on Facebook and Instagram? She makes it sound like the cook-off will be more like WrestleMania, and she's planning on whupping my ass there—which we both know she could do." He smiled at his old friend.

Trinity smirked, "Once again—it's Dawn, remember? She doesn't do calm so just expect big, loud trouble."

"You're right, girl," said Rocky, shaking his head. "But one more thing. You're on my team, right? On Rocky's gumbo team?"

"Sorry, Rocky. I'm not even neutral on this issue. Remember, this is my mom's gumbo recipe too. And as a true Gumbeaux Sistah, I have to insist that it beats your mom's gumbo any day. Besides, Dawn would kill me."

"Calm? Do you not know my sister at all?"

- Trinity

CHAPTER 46

Dawn walked up and down the aisles at the Western Outfitters store looking for just the right gift for Lola. Her conscious was bothering her over her behavior with Bud, so she was trying to buy a guilt-present for her best friend.

When she and Trinity had blasted Bud for the couple's breakup, it had been a spur-of-the-moment decision. True, she had planned on contacting Bud sometime or other to give him a piece of her mind, but the decision to go to his work place had been made when they were accidentally passing by his nursery. At the time, it had seemed like a good one. She had felt like she was defending Lola. It had not helped that she had also been furious about Rocky and the spilled mason jar of gumbo that day.

It turned out not to have been the greatest of ideas. Lola had been upset with her over the whole deal, and her friend felt bad enough over the breakup. Dawn had not meant to add to her problems.

So, the idea of buying Lola a present had come to mind. Dawn thought she might get her something cute at the western clothing store that she could wear to her parents' barbecue.

She considered the selection of women's western shirts, hats, bandanas, and bolo ties, but nothing was speaking to her—until she turned the corner on the last aisle. Dawn knew she had found gold. It was a whole aisle of beautiful cowgirl boots. Perfect! She would buy her friend a gorgeous pair of red leather boots, and all would be forgiven. Lola would love them.

She knew Lola's size—seven—because she and Dawn had once disclosed their shoe size to each other. Dawn still regretted the moment. Once in a while, Lola still liked to make jabs at Dawn and her size ten feet.

"Yes, I know. They're grape stompers," she told her friend ruefully. They were big and not very pretty, despite consistent pedicures. An old boyfriend of Dawn's once had the nerve to laughingly tell her, "Dawn, you're a beautiful women, from the ankles up!" He was a very short-lived boyfriend and probably lucky to be alive at all.

Dawn made the purchase and left with the box tucked under her arm. "My girl is gonna love this! She'll be the second-best-looking woman at the barbecue!" She giggled at her own joke on her way out the door.

CHAPTER 47

Cooper arrived home that afternoon after school, hoping for an empty house. His stepdad, Andre, had been missing for three days, no doubt out on a bender somewhere.

Sometimes, Cooper tried to imagine what it must be like to be Andre. He could not imagine not caring about anything—his house, his job, his reputation, or his kid. But that was the nature of Andre's drinking. He was into the alcohol most of his waking hours, and sleeping with women he had picked up in bars or on the street. He only showed up at home from time to time. He worked construction jobs just long enough to keep the lights on and the liquor cabinet stocked. He never bothered with buying food, but Cooper was able to feed himself from his small wages, his café boss's generosity with leftovers, and the local Food Bank. Cooper's life was hard, but Andre's life seemed like hell.

Of course, Cooper knew what it felt like to be out on the streets himself. During those times when the booze and violence were both front and center at their house, Cooper cleared out and hid somewhere until it blew over or until Andre disappeared again. When in hiding, sometimes the local church helped him, and sometimes his boss at the café did. But sometimes he would be forced to sleep in an open garage in the neighborhood for shelter. He would leave before sunrise and get himself to school where he cleaned up as best he could in the boys' bathroom.

Today, Andre's car was not in the driveway, so Cooper let himself in the through the kitchen door. He dropped his backpack on the counter and helped himself to a cold drink in the fridge. His plans were to grab a shower and a meal right away because he never knew if Andre would show up, and Cooper might have to leave in a hurry. After his shower, he would hit the books for homework and maybe catch a little TV. He headed through the dark living room before heading upstairs to his room.

He knew something was wrong the moment he drew near the couch in the dark room. He felt the trouble before he saw it. Andre rose up off his prone position on the couch like a cobra. He snarled, "Why are you waking me up, you little shit?"

Cooper stopped still and felt his blood go cold. He kept his voice as calm as he could, "Hey Andre. What are you doing here? I didn't see our car out front."

"It's not your car, stupid," came the cold reply. "And I let Sandy borrow it. She's coming to get me later."

Cooper could only imagine who Sandy was, so he shrugged and said, "OK, well, I'm gonna grab a shower." Andre grunted a reply while Cooper took the stairs two at a time and locked the bathroom door.

Later that evening, Cooper had not heard much downstairs, so he emerged from his room to see about food. He had left a couple of tacos in the fridge for his dinner. He found Andre at the kitchen table with a bourbon in one hand and Cooper's tacos half-eaten on a plate.

"Where'd the food come from?" asked his stepfather.

"I bought it on the way home from school," answered Cooper, getting a glass of water and hoping there were some eggs left in the fridge for dinner.

"Where'd you get the money?"

"I've been working some shifts at the Beck n' Call—washing dishes," answered Cooper warily. He did not like the look in Andre's eyes.

"You're working? How much you get?"

"Just a few bucks here and there." Cooper laughed nervously, "Dishwashing doesn't pay as much as it should."

Andre's eyes drew into slits. His voice came out a harsh, whiskey whisper, "Are you smart-assing me?"

Cooper shook his head stiffly, "No, sir. I'm just sayin, they don't pay me much."

"I'm gonna need that money."

"Wait, what? I can't, Andre. I need that money for food."

"Are you kiddin' me, boy?" Andre looked at Cooper sideways, a warning shot. 'I give you a roof over your head and pay the utilities on this dump. What do you do? Now I'm gonna need that money for tonight."

"But . . ." Before Cooper could finish his sentence, a fist shot out and hit him square on the side of his head, knocking him straight to the floor. He heard Andre rising to his feet from his bar stool and knew that could only mean bad news. Andre was a hard man, hardened from years of construction work and mean from years of being good at drinking. Cooper tried to get up and get out of the way, but was too slow in his weak state. Andre kicked him three times—once in Cooper's side, once on his arm, and once in the back of his head. Cooper almost felt himself go out, but held on.

Andre said, "Now, I'm gonna use the john, and when I get back, that money had better be on this counter. I think now you know I mean what I say." He stumbled out of the room, and Cooper knew he had only one chance. Blood and tears wet his face, but he forced himself to stay conscience. He jerked himself up, ignoring the terrible pain in his head and side and made it out the back door.

CHAPTER 48

That evening, Helen sat in her cozy, eclectic living room. One whole wall was filled with bookshelves with volumes covering every topic of nutrition, massage, energy work, meditation, and law of attraction ever written. She was chatting to Bea on her phone with a cup of tea in her hand.

"Bea, the workshop is coming up so fast! I always get a little stressed over these things. I just know I'm going to forget something."

"You've got this, Helen. It's not your first time doing this, and this time, you'll have Cooper there to help you. If anything goes wrong, he can fix it. Just use the slide show to help guide you as you go along, like having an outline on the screen. It will be a piece of cake."

Chimes sounded through the room as the front doorbell rang.

"Was that the doorbell?" asked Bea. "Are you expecting someone? I can let you go."

"No, hold on a second, and I'll see who it is. It's probably my neighbor wanting to borrow my hedge trimmers for her boxwood again. Hers broke, and she said she'd be over."

She opened the door, and Bea heard her gasp.

Helen whispered into the phone, "Oh, he's hurt bad! I'll call you back, Bea."

He leaned against the doorjamb, holding his head. Dried blood was on his face and shirt, and he held his arm as if it would not hold itself up.

"What on earth!" she cried. "Come inside!" She helped him in and to the couch. "Stay put," she said and ran to get him a towel and an ice pack from the freezer.

Cooper looked up at her and Helen could see that his face was severely bruised, and his arm was causing him a lot of pain.

"Were you in fight?" she asked.

"No," he said simply.

"Did your stepfather do this to you?"

"Yeah. I think I may need some help. Can I stay here tonight?"

"Yes, of course. You did the right thing coming here, Cooper."

CHAPTER 49

The next morning Trinity, Judith, Helen, Bea, and Lola were all at Dawn's house, crowded around her kitchen, helping her get ready for the big cook-off. Trinity was putting last-minute touches on a big bowl of potato salad, and Judith tended to a pot of rice. Dawn stirred a whopping pot of gumbo.

Bea and Lola happily sampled the wares while Helen said, "The workshop attendees are going to love having this for lunch tomorrow. I'm so glad we thought to do the cook-off there."

"Good. I need to make the judges very happy, Helen. I want to beat Rocky once and for all in this contest. That big-mouth needs to eat his words."

"The gallery is all ready for the event too. Everything is spick-and-span," said Judith.

"And the press will be there, so that will make it official," said Dawn. "I also invited two local chefs to join in the judging, just to ramp up the clout of the whole thing. Then, after the judges get their gumbo, our doors will open to the public, and people can come in and fill up a cup for five dollars. Safe House is excited to accept the proceeds, so some good will come of it. I mean, other than having Rocky eat his words, although, let's face it, that's the best part," laughed Dawn.

Judith peeked at the dog bed in the kitchen corner where Lucy lay taking a little nap. "Thanks for letting me bring Lucy, Dawn. I'm trying to socialize her, so until her real owners show up, she can come with me into the gallery sometimes. I worry about leaving her at home all day when I have to work."

"She's being good as gold," said Bea. "I don't know why you keep saying she's not well-behaved."

"She's asleep," laughed Lola. "Even Dawn's good when she's asleep."

"Wait till she wakes up," nodded Judith. "But if she starts cutting up too much, I'll put her in the backyard for a bit."

"I've seen her in action, Bea," said Dawn with a grin. "That dog is a hot mess."

"Speaking of dogs, Dawn," said Judith. "Before Lucy showed up, you and I were talking about both of us getting a pup. I don't know when Lucy's owners will show up, but hopefully soon. So are you still looking for one?"

"I talked it over more with Dan, and we decided that we wanted to do a little bit of traveling this year. I've got a couple of wonderful trips in mind and would rather look for a pup after that. Otherwise, we'd just have to board the poor pooch the whole time we were gone."

"I would be happy to watch the dog for you while you travel," said Trinity. "I love dogs."

"I know you do, Sis, but remember when we were kids, and I brought home a little lab-mix puppy somebody gave me at the burger joint?" She turned to the group. "I was so happy to have that dog, but when I got it home, Trinity took one look at that pup, and it was as if I didn't even exist anymore. She spoiled it rotten with snacks, slept with it every night, and even named it. It took exactly five minutes for her to steal my dog. Nope. When I get a dog, she's gonna be *my* dog, and you will never, ever meet her in person!" The sistahs laughed while Trinity pouted.

Then Trinity smiled. "You're right. I've never met your imaginary dog, and I'm already in love with it. Best to keep her away from me. Better yet, maybe we'll all get dogs!"

"Not till my globe-trotting is done," said Dawn firmly. "Then we'll go dog shopping together. Meanwhile—and you'll love this—Dan suggested that I could cool down my wanting-a-dog-phase I'm in by naming our garbage can 'Spot!'"

Lola choked on her gumbo, laughing along with the others. "Wait, does that mean we should name the dishwasher 'Spotless?'"

"How about if we name the stove 'Hot Dog?'" laughed Helen.

At that moment, as if on cue, Lucy woke up and got excited over all the human company. She began barking and jumping all over everyone's legs. Judith scooped her up and put her outside. "See what I mean, Bea?"

While the sistahs talked, Dawn went to the corner of the room and brought out a big box with a red ribbon around it.

"Ooooh," said Judith. "What is this? It's not anyone's birthday, is it?"

"Nope," said Dawn with a grin. "It's a surprise for Lola."

"Me? Uh oh. Wait a minute. OK—what do you want?" said Lola, looking at her friend with a fake frown.

"It's not about what I want. It's about what I did."

"Oh well, that could be just about anything," laughed Lola.

"Look," said Dawn, seriously, "I screwed up when I went and yelled at Bud at his work. My intentions were good—you know that. But my methods might have been off. I upset you, and I wanted to say that I'm sorry."

"What? You're serious. This really for me?" asked Lola, her eyes opening wide.

"Yes. I hope you like them!"

"Them? Hmmm, the plot thickens." She shook the box lightly. "Let's see. What could 'them' be? Are there a bunch of live hand-grenades in here? A pack of live rats? Maybe a package of coffin nails because you'll be the death of me someday?"

"Just open it already."

Lola pulled off the red ribbon and opened the box. She pulled out two polished, bright-red, beautiful boots.

"Do you like them? I bought them for you to wear to the big barbecue! Aren't they perfect?"

Lola looked stunned for a moment, then recovered and said, "Dawn, I love them! You know me so well, sistah! And I have to say, they are the perfect thing for the barbecue! You know you didn't have to do this. Sure, I was ticked at you, but I spend half my life being ticked at you for something or other," she laughed. "But thanks. Seriously, they are gorgeous!"

"Oh, whew," said Dawn, turning to look at Trinity. "Thank goodness she likes them."

"You called it," said Trinity happily.

"Speaking of the barbecue, Lola," said Judith, "Do you think it would be OK if I invited someone to come with me?"

Dawn perked up instantly, and the other sistahs were right behind her. Eyes wide, she asked, "Someone—like a date?"

Judith tried to pull off a casual reply, but was not great at it, "Yeah, a friend, you know,"

"Oh yeah, we know!" crowed Dawn. "Tell us everything! What's his name? Who are his people? What's the sex like?"

Judith actually blushed, but laughed, "Calm down! We've only been out a couple of times . . . "

"You what?!" Dawn interrupted. "And you didn't report in?"

"I'm reporting now. Listen he's a nice guy and his name is Marty. And I don't want to make a big deal out of this, OK? He's just someone I know, and I think he'd be fun to bring to Lola's parents' party."

"Of course, bring him," said Lola.

"Hell yeah, bring him," said Dawn. "We can't wait to meet him!" She winked excitedly at Lola and started to say, "Now tell us everything, Judith!"

But just at that moment, something out the window overlooking the backyard caught Judith's attention. She gasped and rapped loudly on the window overlooking the backyard. She called out, "No, Lucy, no!" Then she ran for the back door.

"Saved by the pug," said Dawn disappointedly.

The sistahs looked out and saw Lucy on the back patio with one of Dawn's flower bulbs in her puppy mouth.

Judith came back inside carrying Lucy, bulb and all. "Well, it's obviously time to go. I'll see y'all at the workshop. Dawn, I'm sorry about the bulb. I'll bring you a replacement. I have plenty—they keep showing up on my back steps."

Helen said quietly, "Wait, just a second, Judith. Before y'all leave, I need to talk to you about something serious."

Judith saw the pensive look on her friend's face and said, "Sure thing." She settled Lucy back down into her dog bed and sat on the floor petting her so she'd stay quiet.

Bea said, "It's about last night, isn't it?"

"Did something happen?" asked Dawn.

Helen told them about finding Cooper on her front doorstep the night before, beaten and in bad shape. "He wouldn't let me take him to the hospital, so I doctored him up as best I could and let him fall asleep on the couch. I think his arm was alright, but who knows. I'm worried about his poor face too—he really took a beating. But this morning when I got up, he was gone. I've left a text message for him, and I've got a call into the school. I'm not sure what to do."

Lola was quiet and thoughtful for a moment, then said, "You know, my mom knows someone who works with foster children. Maybe she can tell you how we can help."

"I think you're right, Lola. I'd better call her. I'm really worried. I don't think he has anyone to help him, and I don't think he trusts the school, so he doesn't talk to them. It's a terrible situation."

"I'll get that contact name for you today," promised Lola.

CHAPTER 50

That night, Judith lay in bed thinking about her friends and the problem Helen was facing. As usual, she turned to the only place she knew to find help when things seemed hopeless. *"Lord, please help Helen and Cooper. He's in so much trouble. And please help Helen find a way to help him. And please help the sistahs find a way to help Helen help Cooper. OK, you can see where I'm going with this. As always—your will be done. I love you, Father. Goodnight and see you tomorrow."*

CHAPTER 51

Helen was awake most of the night worrying about Cooper's injuries, and also whether or not he would show up at the workshop the next morning. So, it was a pleasant surprise when he came walking in the Gumbeaux Sistahs gallery on time and without a word began setting up the computer and equipment. He had added an overly-large pair of sunglasses to his ensemble this morning—with good reason.

Helen fixed him a cup of coffee and a croissant and brought it to him. "How are you?" she asked.

"OK," he mumbled, taking the food hungrily.

"Did you see a doctor?"

"No, I didn't. But when I woke up, I could tell nothing was broken. I'm just bruised and sore as hell, but nothing more. I'll live." he said with a shrug. "I always do."

"Cooper, I know we need to get through this workshop now, but can we talk later? Seriously, I'm worried about you."

"Sure, but let's just get this done, and we'll see. And can you pay me now? I'll stay through the workshop, but you will probably be talking to people afterwards, so let's get it over with."

"OK," she said. "But I do want to sit down and talk afterwards. I think we need to." She handed him an envelope with his money inside.

The gallery began to fill up. Sixteen attendees turned up and found chairs, and Helen walked to the front of the room.

"Welcome to the Growing in Love Workshop" she said and then introduced herself and her assistant Cooper to the attendees.

"Sir James M. Barrie said, 'If you have it, you don't need to have anything else, and if you don't have it, it doesn't much matter what else you have.' Today we're going to talk about that one thing we have to have—the greatest aspect of human life—Love. We will examine the importance of love in our lives and the many types of love that exist."

Cooper began the slideshow and Helen continued.

"How important is love? If not for love, you would not have been in the world—it's what keeps our very species going, generation after generation. True, babies can be conceived without love, but they will not thrive without nurturing, another form of love. Love helps us to be physically, mentally, and emotionally healthy. A lack of love in the form of abuse, stress, loneliness, and deprivation can be linked proportionally to a great number of ailments and diseases. To love someone and be loved by someone is one of the most essential ingredients for human survival. It makes life worth living. It gives us self-worth and esteem. It makes life pleasurable and beautiful. People who have never experienced love in their lives are often aggressive, hostile, and unhealthily emotional. When love exists, a person can better face appalling situations and come through effectively. It connects us with a Higher Power and helps us find peace and enlightenment. Without love, war, and violence would have taken over once and for all. Life without love is mere existence, for love is what makes it worth living.

"So, it stands to reason that the more love we have, the better our lives will be.

"There are many types of love. We're going to talk about seven kinds, including love for people in general which includes empathy, compassion, and forgiveness. Then there's self-love which must be cultivated often before the others in order for them all to function well. There's caretaking, which is the type of love we have for our children, or a friend recovering from surgery, or our aging parents. It's mostly about giving, but we receive through the giving. We have platonic love, which is the kind we have through our friendships which makes us feel valued and positive about ourselves. We have deep connection love, which can include family and spouses and even some friends. We form these deep connections when we've been with a spouse forever. It's a different kind of relationship than passionate love, which is another type. Passion is the love the poets sing about. It's equal parts exhilaration and painful longing. It is intense, exciting, usually short-lived, and can make way for the deeper feelings to emerge. Then, finally, there is our love of God or a Higher Power, if you will, and that is the most important love of all.

"Ask yourself, do you have enough love? Sixty-eight percent of Americans say they need more meaningful love in their lives, and ninety-five percent believe that we need more love in the world. Since love is one of the most basic human emotions, how can it be that so many of us find it lacking in our lives? Love can inspire us to write symphonies and build huge buildings to honor our cultures, but love also leaves us feeling vulnerable and opens us to possible rejection. It requires courage, patience and effort—not an easy task list. Here are some ways to cultivate more love.

"After each suggestion that I make here in the slideshow, we will take a few minutes to write down ways in which you can put this into practice and then have a short discussion period over what we came up with. We'll get some wonderful ideas by brainstorming this way, and we'll learn and lead each other in love."

Helen read through her list and lively discussion ensued between all the attendees. Even a couple of press people, who had arrived early, joined in the exchange.

Helen continued, "OK, number one: Love yourself. Before you can share love with others, you have to feel it for yourself. This will require alone time to develop this love. Focus your intentions on truly loving you and filling yourself up with positive feelings.

"Two: Recognize the things that are holding you back from love. Rumi wrote, 'Your task is not to seek for love, but merely to seek and find all the barriers within yourself that you have built against it.' Perhaps you have been hurt or betrayed by a past relationship, and you fear vulnerability now. Take some time now to write how you feel about giving yourself over to the different types of love. This is an important step to deepening your ability to love.

"Three: Give —just to be giving. A good way to bring love into your life is to give your time and energy to those who need your help. Volunteering offers many opportunities to grow in love. What can you do to give back?

"Four: Practice blessing yourself with meditation. Practice this blessing daily. Say, 'May I be at peace, and may my heart remain open. May I realize my true heart's beauty. May I be healed, and may I be a source of healing this world.' Try this silently now at your seats.

"Five: Open your heart. Try this as a daily routine. Put your hand over your heart and imagine that you are breathing in and out through your heart, gently, slowly, smoothly. With each breath, draw in peace and self-love. Try this at your place now.

"Six: Find love everywhere. As you open your own heart, you will begin to see love everywhere you go. Choose to see it more and more. Let it be your guide. Be motivated by it. You will begin to see that you have always had all the love you need—you just didn't know it. When other people see that you embody love, you will draw even more love to yourself. The world will benefit by your example. Let's take a moment a feel the love in this room. Then examine your daily lives and find the love that existed there all along."

The slideshow was almost at an end, and it was stopped on one last slide that read, "Because the Beatles said it best—Love is all you need."

Helen then told the quiet room, "Take this practice with you today, my friends. Let love guide your life. Let love in. Don't have a smaller life than you deserve."

Those last words floated around the room and hit home with many people, two of them especially. Both Judith and Cooper stood stock-still, deep in thought.

Don't have a smaller life than you deserve.

- Helen

CHAPTER 52

Dawn and Rocky showed up to Helen's workshop at eleven and while Helen spoke, they began to get the gumbo and rice heated up for the cook-off. The sistahs set out bowls, cups, spoons, napkins, and beverages. They served sweetened and unsweetened iced tea. Trinity brought a big batch of her Trinity Cookies to share for dessert.

At a few minutes before noon, Helen thanked her attendees and invited them to take part in the delicious gumbo lunch and explained how the competition would work between Chef Rocky Breaux and Gumbeaux Sistahs Gallery co-owner, Dawn Berard. Each attendee judge was given a ballot. They were not told which gumbo was cooked by whom, but there was a big "A" on Dawn's cookpot and a big "B" on Rocky's. The judges were given ballots that simply had the two letters printed on them—A and B. The judges were to circle the letter of their favorite gumbo and then turn their ballots into Bea. There would be eighteen ballots altogether including the two guest chef judges brought in from local restaurants.

The judges lined up and were given two labeled cups of gumbo each. They took their cups to a table and carefully tasted each entry. Around the room it was dead-quiet, except for the sounds of judges clicking their spoons against the cups and marking their ballots.

After about twenty minutes, all the ballots were collected by Bea, and the tallying began. Bea and Helen were in charge of counting the ballots silently in front of the group, and the suspense began to build. Rocky and Dawn both stood behind the counter and waited anxiously as the ballots mounted up.

Finally, the count was done. Helen and Bea sat for a moment, looking at each other. Their expressions were controlled, but Judith could read the incredulity in their eyes. She wondered, *"Was it that much of a landslide ballot? Why are they looking at each other that way?"* She thought maybe they were hesitant to embarrass Dawn or Rocky. Both of them had reputations on the line.

Bea stood up and cleared her throat, "Uh, OK. We've counted the ballots, and this is truly unexpected, I know, but it seems—*we have a tie!"*

Gasps could be heard all around the room.

"I know it's just crazy, but both Dawn and Rocky got nine votes each!"

A reporter from the Advocate snapped the stunned look on the cooks' faces and jotted down notes.

"What?" was Dawn's delayed, stunned reaction.

"Oh my gravy!" said Rocky, distressed. He turned on Dawn. "Did you steal my recipe?"

"Of course not!" answered Dawn hotly. "Did you steal mine?"

"She didn't, Rocky," said Trinity. "She tried, of course, but she didn't succeed."

"Then what the heck?" growled Dawn. She filled cups with A and B gumbos and tasted for herself. "This is crazy - they're both delicious, and oh my God, of course they are! And guess why? These are both my mom's recipe. I'd know it anywhere!"

Rocky tasted both gumbos too. "Dawn, this is my mom's recipe! She taught me how to make it as a kid, and nobody's gumbo tastes like hers."

"Well my mom's does!" exclaimed Dawn. Rocky and she looked at each other, and a slow realization crept into their eyes, reddening their faces. Trinity beat them to the punch, "Our moms were best friends," She howled with laughter. "It's the same recipe!"

The whole room exploded with laughter, all except Dawn and Rocky, who stood shaking their heads. The reporter from the Advocate was writing and taking pictures furiously with a look of sublime amusement on her face.

"I can't freaking believe this, Dawn," said Rocky, shaking his head.

"Oh my God. It makes sense though. This recipe was not only my mom's," said Dawn. "It was my Grandmother's too. Mom wouldn't have told anyone this secret recipe—except her very best friend. My God, we should have known!"

"Shoot," said Rocky, disgusted. "I really would have liked to wipe the floor with you, Dawn. But you know, now I'm kind of glad it worked out like this."

"Actually, me too," grinned Dawn.

"Your mom was good to me," said Rocky, nodding. "In fact, she was the best. And so were you, Dawn," He grinned shyly.

"You're not such a blockhead yourself, Rocky Breaux."

"I know," he said, then grinned with a gleam in his eye. "But you're still a badass!" Dawn threw up her hands in disgust.

Judith made her way to the front door of the gallery where people waited in line to buy five-dollar-cups of gumbo. The gallery filled up quickly and kept everyone busy.

Helen packed up her workshop materials while talking to some of the attendees. When there was a lull, she looked around to make sure that Cooper had been able to get himself a cup of gumbo while waiting for her. He was nowhere to be found.

CHAPTER 53

The next day, Judith stopped into the local pet store looking for dog treats. She wanted Lucy to be happy while she stayed with her, no matter how short of a time it might be.

She passed by a bin full of soft-looking blankets with animal prints on them. One of them showed images of timber wolves in the wild. They looked fierce and free.

"Lucy would love this comfy thing, and she could probably learn a thing or two from these noble beasts," she thought, chuckling to herself. *"It's probably a waste of money to buy it for her since she'll be leaving soon, right?"*

She nonchalantly ignored that question, threw the blanket in the cart, and went on with her shopping.

CHAPTER 54

Helen dialed the number of the contact given to her by Lola's mother. "Good morning. May I speak to Stacy Smith, please?" she asked the young man who answered the phone at the James Samaritan Center, the local foster care coordinating organization.

A minute later, Helen was talking to the person who could change Cooper's life, one way or the other.

"Call me Stacy, and I'll call you Helen, if that's OK with you. I like to do away with formalities as soon as possible," said Stacy a few seconds into their conversation.

"I'm all for that too," said Helen. She dove right into the reason for her call. After explaining about Cooper's situation, Helen asked, "What could happen to this boy, Stacy? I'm very worried about him."

"It depends on several things, for instance, his age and his situation at home."

"His situation is not good. I've seen what the stepfather does to him. He's beaten the boy up pretty badly, and it's not the first time, either."

"I've been told that the Department of Children and Family Services—or DCSF—is aware of this family and has sent people out there before, but there was no visible evidence of physical harm on the boy at the time, and Cooper always insisted that he was OK. But you get a feel for these things after a while, Helen. I've been worried about him myself."

"Well, there's physical evidence now—a big, fat black eye," said Helen angrily. "What if I could get Cooper to admit to the abuse?"

"That, of course, changes everything right away. He can be removed from the house and placed in foster care."

"Foster care?" asked Helen. "Would he be safe there? Can his stepfather get to him there?"

"Cooper would be placed with a family who would keep him in their home, feed him, make him feel welcome, make sure he gets to school, etc. The courts will take care of the stepfather. With Cooper's help, the stepfather would be arrested and charged. Then he would stay with foster families at least until he ages out of the program. At that point, he will be out on his own. Of course, that can be the hardest thing of all for a young person. Just being out there in the world for the first time in their lives is extremely hard. The truth is, older kids graduating out of the foster program need a great deal of help to make it—just as much as the younger ones do, and there are not many programs to help out there with this problem, although, we do have a decent one that Cooper could possibly take advantage of when the time comes."

"If he goes into foster care, how do you know that the people he is placed with are good folks?"

"Foster parents are fingerprinted and background-checked. Then they have to go through a six-month foster training program."

"Six months . . . that's good," said Helen, thinking out loud. "And that means that not just anyone could take him in, doesn't it?"

"Not until they complete the training." Stacy Smith was used to asking hard questions, so she came straight to the point, "Of course, there are emergency circumstances where exceptions are made. Do you really want to help the boy, Helen?" she asked.

"I would like to try."

"Then go find Cooper, and we'll see what we can do."

CHAPTER 55

The next morning, Helen got in her car and drove to the Beck-N-Call café. She had been home making herself a cup of coffee that morning and wondering how she could get ahold of Cooper since he was not answering her calls or texts. Then she suddenly remembered that Cooper mentioned that he picked up the occasional shift washing dishes there.

She drove up to the side of the café just in time to find him dressed in his usual "NO" shirt and old jeans with an apron with the Beck-N-Call logo on it. He was loading garbage bags into the big dumpster out back.

Helen walked up quietly and said, "Hi, Cooper."

He swung around and regarded her carefully. "What are you doing here?" he asked.

"I've come to see you. Can we talk?"

"What about?" he asked warily. Then before she could answer he said, "Look, I'm sorry I dragged you into this. I just needed a little help that night, but I'm better. Thanks though. I'm finished for the day here and have to get going."

He started to walk away, and Helen hurriedly said, "Look, can we just talk a minute? I need to say something to you. You can spare a second, can't you?"

The boy looked at his feet, then up into Helen's eyes. In addition to his black eye, still clearly visible but beginning to heal a bit, he looked as tired as any soul Helen had ever seen. His face was colorless, and the look in his eyes was all pain. It was all Helen could do not to burst into tears at the look on his face.

"Sure, Ok," he said wearily.

"C'mon," she said, "I want to show you something. Let's walk up the block."

She pulled on his arm to get him moving in her direction, and they made their way silently up the street to the front of the Gumbeaux Sistahs Gallery. Helen pointed to the wooden bench sitting under the crepe myrtle tree in front. "This is what we call a Friendship Bench, Cooper. I only sit here with friends, and it's a good place to say what has to be said. So, shall we?"

He dropped down onto the bench next to her and was quiet a moment. Then he said, "Look, I think I know what you want to say. You think you can help me."

"Well, yes that's right. And I would also like to tell you a little story, if that's alright."

He sighed, "Yeah, OK."

So she started… "I know what it feels like, Cooper," said Helen.

"You know what *what* feels like?" he asked.

"Abuse. Being hurt by people. Being beaten by someone who's supposed to be your family."

The boy looked genuinely shocked, "Someone hurt you, Miss Helen?"

"Yes, they did. My husband. He put me in the hospital several times, and there were many times I probably should have been in the hospital, but he refused to take me."

Cooper was silent for a moment. He nodded. "I know what that feels like. But, why would anyone hurt you? You're a nice, old lady."

Helen hid a little laugh. "Well, I think so too, but he hurt me alright. It didn't make any sense, either. He just did it when the mood would come over him, along with the booze, just like it does with your stepfather. I'd probably be dead now if it weren't for Bea's help. You remember Bea, right?"

"Yeah, I don't think she likes me much," he shrugged.

"You'd be wrong about that. Bea is just tough, that's all. And very protective. But did you know that she prays for you every night?

Well, of course you don't know that. But she does—and so do I. We've both been worried about you."

"Don't worry about me, Miss Helen. I can tough this out. I just have to hang in there so I can have a place to live for a little while. I need a place to stay even if it's bad sometimes. I can handle it though."

"You are a big guy, Cooper, and you might be right that you would be able to take it—on the outside. But nobody, and I mean nobody, can take that stuff on the inside." She said it so fiercely that he looked her in the eye. She had tears there, and looking at her, he was surprised to find himself blinking back a couple of his own.

"I can't picture anyone hurting you like that," he said angrily. "You're such a little thing. Anyone who would do that is completely insane. Where is this idiot now?"

"He's dead, Cooper."

"Oh, well, good then. It couldn't happen to a nicer jerk."

She smiled at him. "Thanks. You know, you might not want to hear this, but I get the strongest feeling in my heart that you are a really good guy."

"Don't give me that," he said. "No one ever says that about me."

"No, listen, my heart is never wrong."

He looked her squarely in the eye. "Thanks, Miss Helen. I guess it's a nice thing to hear." Then he shrugged. "Look, I've really got to go. There's nothing to be done about my situation. If I had that jerk who fancies himself to be my stepfather arrested, I'd be carted off and put in foster care."

"Wouldn't that be better than what you have now?"

"Who knows? I mean, I'm sure there are lots of really good folks who take kids in. I've heard some good stories about the program, but I've also heard bad things can happen to kids who get placed with the wrong people. They end up in just as much trouble as they started out in. One guy I knew from the streets was beaten just as badly by his foster dad as his own stupid family. He's now off the streets, but he's in prison for robbery. He didn't have much of a chance, if you ask me. At least with my stepdad, I know mostly how to hide from him when he's been drinking. And sometimes he disappears for days at a time—those are the best times for me."

"That man belongs behind bars," Helen hissed angrily. "He's a drunken felon using a good, young man as a punching bag."

"But if I have him arrested, then I'm on my way to foster care. None of it sounds good to me. I've just got to hold out till I can get out on my own."

"And then what?"

"I don't know yet. I've got the job washing dishes, and I can maybe get jobs here and there, like I do now, helping people out with their computers."

"Sounds OK. But what about college? You're a smart kid. It would be a terrible shame not to go."

"I can't see that happening. It's hard to keep your grades up when you're homeless half the time. So, I'm pretty sure a scholarship is out. And then how would I eat? Or pay rent? I've gotta be able to take care of myself. And right now, I have other things to think about just till I can get out of school and out from under living with that jerk. Then I can figure something out."

"And when will that be?"

"When I'm eighteen."

"How old are you now?"

"Sixteen—and a half."

"That's another year and a half till you're legal, Cooper. How can you keep doing this for another year and a half?"

"My boss has a room out back where I can bunk for the rest of school if I have to. True, it's kind of creepy in there. The roof leaks, and there's a mouse problem, and I've never seen so many spiders. But still, I've seen worse. There were plenty of times I hid there when the jerk was in that mood."

He was watching her, and it suddenly looked like the sun rose in her face. She was smiling strangely at him and he could tell that an idea had just come into her head. She reached out for his arm. "C'mon Cooper. Let's go talk to some people I know. I know we can do better than a spider-house for you."

"Older kids graduating out of the Foster Care program need a great deal of help—as much or more than the younger ones do."
- Stacy Smith

CHAPTER 56

Judith lay in bed that night, and a prayer came to mind.

"Lord, it occurs to me that you have a pretty wicked sense of humor. That cook-off was a perfect example. In fact, I think you're quite the practical joker—and that was a good one! It wouldn't surprise me to find out that many of your miracles started out as jokes. I'm thinking right now of the parting of the Red Sea. In my mind I can picture you smiling when the Pharaoh was chasing Moses and the Israelites. Then, right before the sea parted, you probably said to some angel friends, 'Just watch this!'

Of course, right after that, Pharaoh's men were demolished by the returning waters. So OK it had a rough ending, but it started out as a pretty good practical joke.

And by the way, Lord, I suspect Lucy might be one of your joke-miracles. I want to thank you so much for having her show up on my doorstep. And meeting Marty has been really very nice too. But I don't know. You and I both know what is bound to happen. I've adjusted to being alone, and you know I do OK with that—as long as I have the sistahs. Maybe I should just leave it like that. I would hate to rock the boat now."

Her thoughts went back over all the lovers and husbands in her past. She remembered the love like it was yesterday, but she remembered the pain quite clearly too. Her heart froze in dread of going through all that again. Then the words of her dear friend Helen at her workshop filtered into her thoughts from nowhere. Those words were clearly spoken for her, even if her friend didn't know it. She'd said, "Don't have a smaller life than you deserve."

Judith was surprised to find a single tear sliding down her cheek in the dark of her bedroom.

"Lord, I'll admit I'm scared. I don't know what's going to happen, but please, don't let me get demolished by the Red Sea.

And Lord, please help Helen help that boy, Cooper. I don't know what needs to happen, but it sounds like he needs you right about now. And so does Helen.

Still, I thank you. As always—your will be done. I love you, Father. Goodnight and see you tomorrow."

"Just watch this!"
- God

CHAPTER 57

Early in the morning, Bea met Helen in front of the Covington Police Department. The two women pushed their way through the glass door to the main entrance. Bea held it open for her friend.

"Thanks for coming with me to get fingerprinted, Bea."

"No problem," said Bea. "Do they throw you in the slammer after they take your prints?"

Helen giggled then said in her best old-movie-gangster voice, "No, Bugsy, they'll never take me alive! You dirty rat, you're not going to squeal on me, are you?"

Laughing Bea confirmed, "Don't worry, they won't get a thing out of me, dear."

Later that afternoon, Helen, Bea, Cooper, Father Jim, and Stacy Smith from the James Samaritan foster care agency, and Jody Tyler from the DCFS stood in front of Judge Ernest Sloane's desk in his courthouse chamber.

"Are you Helen Hoffmann?" he asked.

"Yes, your honor."

"And are you Cooper Landry?"

"Yes sir."

"Ms. Smith and Ms. Tyler, we've met before.

"Yes, Judge Sloane," they answered.

"OK, let's see here. You are petitioning to have an emergency placement today. Ms. Hoffmann is willing to take Mr. Landry into her home. No other close relatives can take Cooper while we figure out his living situation, Ms. Smith?"

"No, sir," she said, "There is no other family that we've found so far."

"I see that you've done the fingerprinting and also registered for the Foster Care classes, Ms. Hoffmann. That's good. And you've provided us with an impressive list of personal references, including one from the good Father Jim here. Jim, how are you? Your Sunday sermon was particularly good this week."

Father Jim smiled, "Thanks, Ernie. It was good to see you in church as usual. And I want you to know that you won't find better people than Helen Hoffmann—and she has a whole slew of amazingly good women friends in the community to back her up."

"That's good to hear. So, please explain the emergency part of this to me, Ms. Tyler."

"We felt that Cooper needed to be removed from his house immediately, sir. There's been physical and emotional abuse, and the young man has been forced many times to run from the home himself while the stepfather, Andre Dupre, is in residence. Mr. Dupre himself is violent and abuses alcohol and disappears from home for days at a time, leaving Cooper without food or care. In fact, he is missing from the home at this present time. It is our opinion that it's a completely unsafe environment, and a placement is in order."

"But an emergency?" asked the judge.

"Yes, Judge, as you can see by the bruises on Cooper's face – he's being physically abused in the home and that makes it a mandatory removal. But you see, Helen hasn't had time to complete the foster care classes, as is required to become a foster parent. She actually only just found out about the classes, but she registered immediately when she did. Now truthfully, we could place Cooper in another home, but we believe that because Helen wants to take Cooper in and they know each other well—he's actually worked for her in the past; he's very good with computers, sir—that it would be a happier space for Cooper right now."

"Good to hear that. But what I really want to do is hear from Cooper. What do you have to say about this placement, son?"

Cooper looked carefully at the judge and back at Helen. "Judge, Miss Helen's the only one who has ever given a damn about me. She's the real deal. She cares. May I please go with her?"

"Of course, we will monitor the situation carefully too and report back to you, your honor," said Ms. Tyler.

The judge looked into the pleading face of the boy who had seen too much for his years already. Then he looked at the sweet, earnest face of the little Gumbeaux Sistah, standing and wringing her hands nervously.

"I'm going to give my consent to this placement, folks. It feels like the right thing to do. Someone gave me a break when I was a boy, Cooper, and it made all the difference in my life. Miss Helen, take care of Cooper. He's going to need a friend. Cooper, be good to Miss Helen—she obviously is willing to go the extra mile for you."

The judge saw a light come into the boy's eyes and felt the need to quickly turn away and pretend to adjust his robes as he wiped his own eyes. He knew he had just witnessed a turning point moment in a young life.

After papers were signed and they were dismissed, the group filed out of the courthouse, and there was not a dry eye among them.

CHAPTER 58

"I need one more pushpin," said Dawn, standing on a step stool in Helen's guest bedroom.

"OK, here you go, but hurry up. They'll be here any minute!" said Lola anxiously.

Dawn shoved the pin in the wall and stepped down while Lola, Judith, and Bitsy did a last-minute tidying up in the little room.

The doorbell rang just as Judith was saying, "It looks great, sistahs. Y'all do good work!" Then she hurried down Helen's hallway, yelling, "He's here!"

She opened the door, and in walked Cooper, Helen, Bea, Father Jim, and Ms. Smith, and Ms. Tyler.

Judith walked up to the young man, smiling. "Welcome, Cooper."

"Thanks," he said sincerely. Then he turned and said "And thanks, all of you. I really appreciate all this and all of you. Thanks for making this happen."

"Our pleasure, Cooper," said Ms. Smith.

"Remember, you can call me anytime if you need me and I'll be checking in with you soon," added Ms. Tyler.

All at once a ruckus sounded from the end of the hall, and all the remaining sistahs flew out of the guest room. "Hi!" called Dawn, walking straight up to the young man and taking his hand. "There's a bunch of us here, but we're not all staying. We don't want to drive you crazy on your first day, but we did want to welcome you."

"And we couldn't resist helping Helen fix up your room for you," said Lola. "Come and see!"

Cooper looked at Helen, and she said with a laugh, "Go ahead and look, or they'll never leave."

He carried his suitcase down the hall and into the little room which was freshly painted a light blue. There was a queen-sized bed and a nearby dresser. The closet held a bunch of new hangers. The nightstand held a new reading lamp. A wooden desk was in another corner and new, dark-blue bedspread and pillows were on the bed. Everything felt clean, fresh, and inviting.

"This is really nice," he said shyly.

"The sistahs helped clean this all up, and it's all yours now—but the poster was my idea," said Helen with a grin.

On the wall over the bed, held up by pushpins, was a large, black poster with a single word printed on it in bold, white letters that simply said, "YES."

"Ha!" he said and looked at Helen with a glint in his eyes. "That's great!"

"He likes it," thought Helen, *"That's all that matters."*

Dawn, who was bursting with excitement, shouted out, "We're your new aunties!"

"OK, must be time to go," said Bea, laughing and scooting her friends towards the front door. "Don't mind them. You don't have to deal with these crazy women. At least, not today."

He turned his face away from her, but Helen could have sworn that she saw a smile. "I could use some aunties," he said.

Helen grinned up at the tall boy. "I'm glad you're here. I think you're going to be alright."

"I think we'll both be alright, Miss Helen," he said softly.

Helen left the room before he could see the happy tears that sprang into her eyes. *"Thank you, Father,"* she thought, *"Who knew this kind of happiness could come to me at this time of my life? Well, I guess you did."* She smiled through her tears, dabbed at her eyes, and then called out loudly, "Cooper, I'm going to make you some gumbo!"

CHAPTER 59

On Saturday morning, the day of Lola's parents' barbecue, Marty picked up Judith at her house. He also had another guest in the car. When Judith had invited him to go with her, he asked if she thought it was alright for him to invite someone else too.

"I feel funny asking, but it's Nancy, my grandniece. She's in town for the week, and I might have mentioned that she's thinking of moving here and looking for a job. She's staying with her grandparents in town for a little bit. I thought it would be good to introduce her around a little and the barbecue seems like a good opportunity. It might help her make up her mind. Her grandmother could come pick her up after a couple of hours to save us the trip back."

After Judith cleared it with Lola, she told him, "Of course, bring her along. It's a good idea. Lola's family are good people for her to meet. They're so nice, and they know everybody in town. They'd be a good connection for her."

Nancy was in the backseat when Judith hopped into the car. She was a pretty, young woman in her mid-twenties with long, brown-black hair and dark, striking eyebrows.

"Goodness," said Judith, "Your uncle didn't tell me how pretty you are! How are you enjoying Covington so far, Nancy?"

"It's so beautiful here, and everyone has been great to me. Thanks for letting me traipse along with you and Uncle Marty. My boyfriend, Ronnie, lives here, and we wanted to look for jobs in the same town. His parents are from here too."

Judith looked at the young woman and could not help but think, *"She looks so familiar. A movie star? Maybe Elizabeth Taylor? It's her coloring—all that dark hair and pale skin. I can't quite place who she reminds me of. Oh well, I guess it will come to me."*

They arrived at the Trahan home which abutted their original nursery business in Bush, Louisiana. There were quite a few cars parked there already. A lot of people were invited every year, and it was always a good party. They saw tables and a bandstand set up on the side of the commercial building overlooking several acres of nursery stock. Trahan Nurseries had grown from a small family operation started by Lola's grandparents, and now included three nurseries and many employees. It supplied other nurseries, shops, and groceries with wholesale plants and flowers.

Lola walked up to the new arrivals in jeans, a western shirt, and her new red boots.

"Oh, you've got the boots on!" said Judith, grinning. "They look wonderful on you." She introduced Lola to Marty and Nancy.

"So there you are!" Lola said to Marty. "The sistahs have been wanting to meet you." She laughed and turned to greet Nancy. She startled slightly and stared at the girl for a moment.

"I know," said Judith. "Nancy, forgive us, but you look just like Elizabeth Taylor, I think. Doesn't she, Lola?"

"Oh yeah," said Lola. "I couldn't place it at first. I just knew you looked so familiar. But that must be it." Then she said, "I'm glad you came, and I think you're going to have some fun today. My parents know how to throw a party. The band's gonna start any minute—oh, and here comes mom and dad now."

Lola's parents welcomed them warmly. They hugged Judith as if they had known her for years because she was now a Gumbeaux Sistah, along with their daughter. The Trahans told Judith, Marty, and Nancy to please make themselves at home and help themselves to food and drinks. Marty told Lola's father, Fred, that Nancy was new in town and possibly looking for work in marketing. He promptly spirited her off to talk to one of Lola's brothers, who ran the business operation, to see if he could help her out.

With some effort, Bitsy walked up, struggling with a huge, white box. "Help!" she said. "And don't drop it! I promised Lola I'd make my Praline Layer Cake for the party. It's the biggest one I've ever made. It should feed a whole slew of these barbecue fans."

"Come on, Bitsy. I'll help you over to that table. Let's get this all set up," said Judith.

"Wait, I'll help," said Dawn as she, Trinity, and Trinity's husband, Harry, walked up behind them. But before she reached for the box, Dawn grabbed Marty into a big bear hug, "I know who you are! So glad you're here!"

Marty was flustered by the force of nature called Dawn for a moment, but managed to squeeze out with a laugh, "You have to be Dawn. I'm so glad to meet you too!"

Lola interrupted their love-fest, "Hi, everyone. Good to see you, Harry. So, Dawn, notice anything?"

Dawn looked her up and down and then shouted, "The boots! I almost forgot! You wore them! OK, now I know I'm forgiven."

"I'll forgive you if you help get this cake to that table without it landing in the dirt. It's heavy!"

"Here, give it to us, Bitsy. Trinity and I are old hands with anything food-related," laughed Dawn. "Anything at all—moving it to tables, cooking it, and especially eating it!"

"Let me help," said Rocky, suddenly at their side. "Lola, thanks for the invite. I brought my sister Annie from Covington. We're going to start a dance contest, and we'll beat the pants off of any moves that Dawn can put out."

"What? You think you can beat me at a dance-off now? You are so reality-challenged, my friend. You know I can dance your face off and always could."

"So, you accept the challenge?"

"Oh dear Lord, stop already!" said Trinity, disgusted. "Haven't you had enough of contests? What do we have to do to get you to stop? Wait, I know. I'll call this contest a tie too—even before it starts!"

Judith laughed, "Oh, let her dance her legs off, Trinity. It might keep her out of trouble. Probably not, we but can always try."

Bea and Helen walked up through the growing crowd with Cooper tagging along behind them. "What did I hear about dancing? Hey, everyone," said Helen, smiling. To Bea she said, "Did you hear that, Bea? We're going to be dancing our legs off!" She laughed and said to the group, "Ever since Bea started dancing a few years back, you know Bea always wins the dance contests. Get ready to be challenged, Dawn!"

To Cooper she said, "Cooper, say hello to…just everyone."

But before he could say a word, Dawn, Lola, Judith, and Trinity grabbed him in a playful group hug. He laughed and shook his new aunties off saying, "Is it going to be like this every time I see you all?"

"Count on it!" said Judith.

Dawn asked him, "Hey, Cooper, how's it going? Are you and Helen getting along?"

Helen and Cooper looked at each other and smiled. "Oh, well, if only she could cook." His eyes twinkled merrily, and he patted his stomach. He had already put on a few needed pounds under Helen's loving ministrations and was looking healthier.

"Oh yeah? Well, if only he knew the meaning of 'dirty socks go in the hamper!'" she retorted. Their gentle teasing brought a measure of comfort to the sistahs, who collectively heaved a sigh of relief for the two of them.

Lola interrupted, looking at her watch, "I'll be right back. I think mom needs me for a second."

"Do you need help?" asked Dawn.

"No, the band is just about to start. You and Rocky kick off the dancing and get the party started." Lola scurried off towards her parents' house.

Helen asked, looking around, "Now where did Bea get to? I wanted her to show me some of her new dance moves. She just won a new trophy, you know."

Trinity answered, "She's probably just visiting the little cowgirl's room."

"Bitsy is MIA now too. I think she must still be fooling with that big, amazing cake she brought. Did you see it, Cooper?" asked Helen.

"No, but I can't wait to have a piece. And I really can't wait to hit the buffet line! The food looks pretty awesome." he said.

Then, right on cue, the band started up with a country song, perfect for a Louisiana barbecue. Marty swung Judith out on the dance floor and started right in on an expert two-step.

"C'mon, Rocky, if we can't compete with each other, we can at least show 'em how it's done," Dawn said over the music.

"OK, c'mon Badass gal, let's do it," grinned Rocky.

The band played for a couple of songs before Dawn suddenly spotted a familiar face in the crowd.

"I don't freakin' believe it," said Dawn, speaking slowly and staring. She suddenly grabbed Trinity, who was standing nearby, and turned her whole body in the newcomer's direction, pointing. Trinity spotted him immediately. "What the . . . it can't be!"

"No," said Dawn, scowling. "It can't, but it is. And I'm going to do something about it." She stalked away with Trinity right on her heels.

"Bud Broussard!" shouted Dawn. "If I didn't see it for my own eyes, I'd never dream a person could have such gall! What do you think you're doing here?"

Bud looked cornered and did not say anything for a moment. Then he shrugged and said, "Lola's dad needed to talk to me about something, so I came over."

"Well, great timing as usual! Lola's father is in the office. Just go, and don't you dare let Lola catch you here. It'll ruin her whole day!" yelled Dawn, pointing to the office.

Bud put up both his hands protectively and hurried off.

"No way is he going to ruin our girl's parents' big party. I'll chase him down the river if I have to," muttered Dawn, narrowing her eyes.

"He looked scared, Dawn," said Rocky, walking up. "Now that's the girl I know and love." He grinned up at her.

"I can still chase you down the river too, Rocky Breaux," she laughed. "Come on, grab your sister, and let's go hit the gumbo line and see how it measures up!" They joined Marty, Nancy, and Judith who were already at the barbecue station.

The band played, and people filled their plates for the next quarter hour. Then Lola's dad went up on the bandstand and took hold of a mic.

"Folks, my family and I are so happy you could make it today. This is a very special day for us. It's our twenty-fifth annual barbecue. Can you believe that?" A big cheer went up from the guests, and he continued, "We've got something special planned for you this year—a bit of a surprise, you might say. So, let's get it started!" He signaled to the band who started playing the beginning of a song, and suddenly onto the stage walked Bitsy with a mic in her hand. Judith, Dawn, Trinity, and Helen gasped. Rocky said, "Isn't that your friend?"

"What's she up to?" asked Helen, confused.

Bitsy opened her mouth, and an amazing bluesy sound came flying out, singing *Call me* by Blondie.

The sistahs' mouths dropped and their chins almost hit the dirt. "What the . . . . ?" said Dawn.

"Man, she's really good," nodded Cooper appreciatively.

"Who knew?" asked Helen, amazed. She and Dawn looked at each other and burst out laughing. "Where has she been hiding this?" asked Judith.

Bitsy finished her song to loud cheering and catcalls, and Lola's dad took the mic again. "Many of you didn't know that Bitsy Rogers could sing, but, obviously, she doesn't just sing—she rocks! You can find her and her band every Friday nights at Ruby's Roadhouse."

"She has a band!?" said Judith loudly.

Bitsy began again, this time pointing to the sistahs in the audience and said, "Hey sistahs, surprise!"

Dawn whistled loudly, and Helen shouted, "Atta girl, Bitsy!"

After her song, Lola's father took the stage again and said, "I know y'all were so surprised to see our Miss Bitsy singing her heart out up here. Isn't she amazing—let's give her another hand!"

The crowd hooted and clapped, and he broke in after a minute, saying, "Well, we have one more surprise for you today, and I think you'll agree it's a doozie!"

At that point, Bea walked on stage and took the mic while Lola's dad backed away.

"Oh my gravy, does your friend Bea sing too?" asked Rocky.

Dawn just stared at Bea and wondered out loud, "Wait—does she? At this point I don't even know!"

Helen giggled next to her, "I'm not sure either, but I love surprises!"

She was not disappointed.

From out of the main office door, stepped Bud. He strode purposefully towards the stage.

"What's going on? I thought I got rid of him!" said Dawn, frowning.

Bud stepped up onto the stage wearing a black tuxedo.

"Good Lord!" said Judith, "Why is he dressed up like that?"

"Do you think maybe he's going to tap dance?" said Trinity, confused.

Bud signaled the band who started playing a familiar tune.

Then, arm in arm with her parents, Lola stepped out of the main house and walked towards the stage. That was when Judith, Helen, and Trinity lost it and screamed. Rocky kept muttering, "Oh my gravy!" Dawn, for once, was speechless.

Lola wore a long, white gown, a simple, short veil, and—red cowgirl boots. She carried white magnolias straight from the Trahan garden in the backyard. When she reached the stage, Bud helped her up the steps then took the mic from Bea.

"Friends and family, forgive us," he said with a grin. "We just wanted to surprise you, and I think we pulled that off, am I right? Today, Lola and I wanted to be surrounded by the people we love, in a place we love. We didn't want all the bother that can come with a wedding. We don't need any gifts or fuss—not at our age," he laughed. "Everything and everyone we need and want is here with us today. So please, take a few minutes to help us celebrate. Lola Trahan has agreed to marry me today. And I'm marrying her right back."

With that, he handed the mic back to Bea who said, "Dearly Beloved . . . "

The sistahs all had tears streaming down their cheeks. Trinity kept whispering, "This is so romantic. I can't stand it. I'm just gonna have to get married again."

Her husband Harry, who was standing next to her, whispered, "I sure hope it's to me, right?" He grinned at her then added, "Will you wear red boots? I could get into that." He winked. Trinity laughed softly and elbowed him.

After the short and sweet ceremony, Bitsy jumped back on stage, and the band played a joyous rendition of *Chapel of Love* by the Dixie Cups. Everyone in the crowd sang along. *"Goin to the chapel and we're, gonna get married!"* There were plenty of happy tears and smiles.

Dawn made her way over to the couple. "Oh Lola, I can't believe you did this. I'm so happy for you. But I could just kill you too! Do you realize how much I could have helped? I would have done the flowers, and catered, and hired the band, and decorated the whole yard—maybe the street too. And hired a white carriage, and had doves fly over—maybe the Blue Angels too—and . . . skydiving!"

Lola laughed and hugged her friend, "Dawn, you are my best friend, but that's why I didn't tell you. First of all, I could not wait to see the look on your face today—and it was priceless! But secondly, Bud and I really just wanted something very simple, and something people could just show up for and enjoy along with us, without a lot of fuss."

"Well, you got me. I don't think I've ever been more surprised in my life." She turned to Bud sheepishly. "Bud, I'm so sorry. Don't hate me. This whole time I thought you were a rat, but you were actually a prince helping Lola pull off a wonderful surprise. Who knew? And to think I almost threw you out of your own wedding!"

"Don't worry, Dawn, it made me realize how lucky Lola is to have such a good friend that she would punch the lights out of anyone who crossed her, which, believe me, won't ever be me." He laughed merrily, but was also dead-serious.

Dawn hugged him hard and whispered, "Take care of our girl. And just so you know, now I'd punch the lights out of anyone who crossed you too."

Bud laughed, but Lola said seriously, "No, she means it."

Then Lola grinned up at him with a mischievous twinkle in her hazel eyes and said, "Hold on, I have one more little surprise." She took off up onto the stage again.

"What is it?" Dawn asked Bud.

"Beats me," he said. "This is a mystery to me too."

Lola found the mic on its stand, leaned into it, and looking fondly out at her new husband, said, "This one's for Bud." She walked back by the drummer and came back to the mic carrying her old brass saxophone. Then she threw her white veil back over her shoulders, leaving her bare arms out and wrapped around her old instrument. She stood up tall on the stage with her white dress hiked up, blowing in the breeze, and brushing the tops of her red boots. Then she threw herself into the music and wailed out the sweet tune of *Just the Way You Are* by Billy Joel.

Bud watched her and looked like he was falling in love all over again.

When she finished, the crowd went crazy, and she walked back to Bud while the band picked up playing again.

He took her hand and kissed it tenderly, "Wife, I think we should take those red boots out for a spin, don't you?"

"You're on, husband," grinned Lola.

The band played, and the crowd danced and cheered the couple's second First Dance in their married lives. Everyone wished them a joyous life to their faces, and in their hearts.

If ever a collective prayer for happiness was heard, that one came through loud and clear.

CHAPTER 60

Several hours later when the crowd started to thin out, Lola's father stood with her at the edge of the party and kissed his daughter on her cheek. She beamed happily at him. "Thanks for the great wedding, dad. It's the best one I ever had."

He held onto her shoulders for a moment and looked into his daughter's eye, seeing the happiness there. "Anytime, my sweet girl." Then he hugged her hard.

Behind them Judith, Marty, and Nancy walked up, and Nancy said with a laugh, "This is the best wedding I've ever been to! And guess what, Lola? I think your brother is going to offer me the Marketing job. I mean—what a day! My boyfriend, Ronnie, is going to flip out when I tell him. Thank you for letting me come. And thanks for suggesting it, Uncle Marty."

A female voice hailed them from behind, "Marty? Nancy, is that you? I came to pick you up. I didn't realize this was a wedding!"

They all turned around in time to see an attractive brunette coming out of the parking lot thirty feet away. When she saw their faces, she stopped short and stared.

"Hi Grandma Lillian," called Nancy. "Come and meet everyone."

Lola and Judith looked at each other in horror. "Did you know?" whispered Lola.

Judith shook her head, and a deep, cutting dread settled over her. *"Oh boy,"* she thought, *"Here comes the Red Sea."*

Lillian, stunned, walked towards them. "Lola Trahan, is that you? This is your wedding?"

"Yes, it is."

"Whoever did you get to marry you?" Lillian sneered.

"Bud Broussard," said Lola with a measure of satisfaction after Lillian's Facebook stunt.

"Will wonders never cease," she raised her eyebrows and turned towards her brother who had his arm around Judith. Her surprised expression turned to one of sheer horror. "Judith, what do you think you're doing? Marty, do you know who that is? Wait, this can't be happening—am I having a stroke?"

"Lillian, what are you talking about? This is Judith, the woman I told you about," said Marty, completely puzzled.

Lillian's face turned bright red, and she looked like was just about to create the biggest scene ever created at a nice wedding, when Lola interrupted her, "Lillian, before you say anything, you might want to consider your lovely granddaughter Nancy here and the fact that my brother just offered her a job at Trahan Nurseries. A good job, Lillian. A really good one."

"I'm absolutely thrilled, Grandma!" said Nancy, grinning like a kid at the circus.

Lola went on, "I'm sure she's pleased as punch for you, Nancy. She'll also be pleased to know that Bitsy will not be needing any extra stress at her job at the museum anymore. Do we understand each other, Grandma Lillian?" Lola leveled a look at Lillian that spoke volumes.

Lillian paused and looked with a squinting, struggling look on her reddening face at each and every one of them. She took a long slow breath and squared her shoulders. "Shall we go, Nancy? You can tell me all about your day in the car." She put her arm around Nancy, and together they quickly made their way back to the parking lot. Lillian looked back over her shoulder at her bother and called out sharply, "Marty, we really need to talk."

Judith repeated the sentiment, "Marty, we need to talk, too." He nodded in agreement.

CHAPTER 61

That evening, Marty dropped off Judith at her house. She had to finish up a commissioned painting for a deadline the next day and expected to be painting late into the night. He promised to call her, and they could talk later that evening.

He picked up a light Thai dinner and brought it back to his hotel. The first bite was halfway to his mouth when his phone rang. Seeing that it was his sister, he sighed, put down his fork and thought, *"Oh well, might as well get this over with."*

"Hello, Lillian."

Lillian launched right in with her tirade, "Did you know who she is, Marty? Is that why you wouldn't tell me her name?"

"Calm down, Lillian, so we can talk, OK?" he said, shaking his head. "And no, I didn't know you two had a history—or that you even knew each other. Judith told me on the way home that she used to work for you at the museum. We're supposed to talk about everything a little later tonight."

"Good. I'm glad I'm getting to you before she has a chance to lie to you. First of all, don't believe anything that woman says. And you have to be careful, Marty. Those friends of her are all thick as thieves. If you make a misstep here, it will probably cost Nancy her new job at the Trahan Nurseries."

"I'm sure everything will be fine, Lillian. And are you sure I really need to know anything about this at all. Seriously, how bad could it be? Judith is a very nice person."

"Oh brother, she's already got you bamboozled! Oh yeah, she's nice alright. She was nice enough to help get her replacement at the museum thrown in jail!"

"Really? On what charge?"

"Oh, never mind all that. It's a long, sad story, and most of it was rumors anyway. But it left the museum without a manager. And speaking of rumors, there were plenty going around that she was having affairs—not only with one of our board members, but with my own husband. Jack and I went through a terribly bad patch over that one."

"That doesn't sound good at all," said Marty, a worried crease forming in his brow.

"And then there was her *coup de grace* when she purposefully stole all of the museum's clients the night of our big Spring Fling fundraiser. She and her cronies just whisked them all away down to their new Gumbeaux Sistahs Gallery that night. It nearly devastated the museum, Marty."

"Why would she do that?" he asked, puzzled.

"The woman is my sworn enemy, that's why. The museum board had to fire her because of her incompetency, and she never got over it. And she's probably using you to get back at me, Marty. I wouldn't put it past her. You need to run away and fast—that woman is dangerous."

Marty rubbed at his forehead and closed his eyes against the beginning of a headache.

"Look, Lillian, it's getting late, and I have a lot to think about. I'll get back to you tomorrow about all this. It's a lot to take in, and I'm wiped out."

"OK," said Lillian, sounding disappointed. She was hoping to rile him up more than he obviously was. She would try again later. "Goodnight. I love you, Marty."

"I love you too, Sis," he said and hung up.

He pushed aside his cold dinner. He no longer had an appetite. Looking around the room, his head held a mass of thoughts and questions that needed answers, and he made a decision.

He picked up the phone again and dialed a number, "Hey, I just got off the phone with my sister. I know you have a deadline tonight, but I really need to talk to you. Do you think I could come over? I'm not sure I can sleep tonight until I get some things straightened out."

CHAPTER 62

Judith opened her front door and ushered Marty straight back into the kitchen where she had a pot of decaf started.

"Don't worry about my deadline," she said. "When we got off the phone, I emailed that client and pushed it back later in the week. She was fine with it. I don't usually like to do that, but this is important."

"I'm glad you think so too. There's too much going on here and it's complicated as hell. And I really need some answers. Lillian made some pretty crazy accusations about you, and I just can't wrap my head around the idea that the woman I'm falling for could be Lucretia Borgia in real life. That's how she made you sound, but that just can't be right. Help me out, Judith." He told her the accusations that Lillian had spelled out.

Judith did not know whether to be more stunned over the way Lillian was attacking her or over the fact that Marty just admitted that he had feelings for her. The latter sent a thrill straight down her spine, but the former made her blood boil. She would probably have a stroke if they did not talk this out—and fast.

"Listen Marty, it's no secret that Lillian and I have had a rocky past. A very rocky one. And all over a stupid misunderstanding about me having an affair with her husband—which absolutely did not happen. by the way. But she believed it did at the time. She made my life hell at that museum job. Then, she got the board to fire me because she told them I was incompetent and couldn't reach my fundraising goals. But she herself raised the goals to a ridiculous level that no one could do without a lot of groundwork. Of course, she didn't give me the time or notice to do the groundwork, so I was sunk. She called it incompetence and bullied the board into firing me.

"And I hate to say this, but the whole time all this was going on, she wasn't exactly Miss Innocent in the love relationship department herself. However, I'll be darned if I'm going to be the one to tell you about that. But if she's having trouble with her husband, then the blame is a lot on her. All I'll say is - ask her about my replacement at the museum sometime." Judith shook her head, remembering.

"But I will admit to stealing the museum's clients at the Spring Fling fundraiser. I didn't really want to hurt the museum, but Lillian had just pushed me too far. She even tried to sabotage our gallery opening night. We weren't sure if our little stunt to steal the clients would even work, but it did beautifully, and we lured them down to our gallery like the pied piper. Marty, your sister put me through hell and then almost ruined me financially. There is no love lost between us, believe me. Having said that, I understand if you want to call whatever this is off. It's been really nice knowing you, though."

Marty stared at her, then let out the breath he had been holding, "Wow," he said. "A lot goes on in this little town!"

Judith could not help but grin. "Well it's been quite a year. I thought Lillian had calmed down by now over the whole thing, to tell you the truth. Losing my museum job turned out to be one of the best things that ever happened to me because of the friends I've made and then opening the gallery. I know I was becoming a little more receptive to her. One of the Gumbeaux Sistahs, Bitsy, still works for Lillian, and so it brings us in contact with each other occasionally. I thought things were getting a little better. But it looks like Lillian doesn't feel the same way. Maybe she's not willing to let bygones be bygones yet. Just recently, she went after Lola and Bud. She tried to make everyone on Facebook think she had kissed Bud at this bar. Her plan backfired though because Lola didn't fall for it. But obviously Lillian was trying."

"Oh boy," said Marty. "Look, I have to say—I love my sister, I really do. But she has always been high-strung and dramatic. And a little out of control. When we were in high school together, people knew not to cross her. She fought dirty. I remember she ran for class president one year, and she filled her rival's locker with a roadkill possum. It smelled unbelievably horrible. There were no witnesses, but everyone knew she did it. I think they kind of admired her for it because she actually won the election. That's the other thing—Lillian usually gets her way. I've had plenty of practice living with her, and Lola had the right idea—just don't let her get to you if you can. But I can see she's still a challenge. Kissing, Bud, huh? Are you sure?"

Judith whipped out her phone and showed him the post of Lillian and Bud in a lip lock. "Yep, that's my sister alright. Still a dirty fighter."

"Marty, I didn't know she was your sister, or we probably would never have gotten together. It would have just seemed impossible. But dammit, I like you. I think I'm willing to not let her get to me. I'm willing to tiptoe around all this craziness if you think you can calm her down a tad and are willing to tiptoe with me."

He looked at her smiling, loving, inviting eyes and pulled her to him with a grin, "Well, I'm no ballerina, but let's see what we can do."

CHAPTER 63

That night, Lucy settled into her bed with her new wolf blanket, and Judith snuggled down with a light down-comforter. She turned out the light on the side table, and as usual, a prayer sprang into her head. *"Father, please bless Lola and Bud and bring them deep, lasting happiness for their rest of their lives. It was a beautiful wedding, wasn't it? And Lord please help Marty see past his crazy sister's motives. I probably shouldn't call her crazy when I'm talking to you, but you know what I mean. And Lord, thank for all the love I've known in my life—my children, my family, my friends, and now this crazy dog, Lucy. All these loves are what my whole life has been made up of. All these loves—and especially yours, Lord. As always—your will be done. I love you, Father. Goodnight and see you tomorrow."*

"There's so much love in this place."

- Bea

CHAPTER 64

On Friday night, all of the Gumbeaux Sistahs, Bud, and a pug named Lucy were gathered at the gallery. The 'Closed' sign was on the door, and Dawn and Judith both had their feet up on a low table and were leaning back in their chairs.

"Bitsy's band starts at eight," said Lola. "But I think we have time for a cocktail before we go. Can you believe that girl, by the way? All this time she's been sneaking out on Friday nights to sing at Ruby's, and she didn't mention a thing! I can't believe what a great singer she is."

Judith said, "I remember how she used to tell me that she sang in her church choir back in California years ago. At the wedding she told me that she had to find some way to release the stress she was under from working for Lillian. Yesterday she told me it was odd but since the wedding, Lillian has eased up on her a little. She's not working Bitsy so hard suddenly." She added loudly with a wink to her friend, "Funny thing about that, don't you think, Lola?"

"Well, I can't wait to hear her again," said Dawn. "So, what kind of cocktail are you making over there, Lola?"

Lola was rummaging around in their liquor cabinet, trying to make drinks for everyone. "We are really low on stock here. We just have odds and ends to work with. I'll have to invent something for us before we head on out to Ruby's."

A few minutes later she produced a brownish-reddish concoction in martini glasses and said, "OK, I'm calling this one 'The Gumbeaux Sistahs Kitchen Sink Cocktail.' It's got everything in it but the . . ."

Bud and the Sistahs laughed and tasted it. Bud said, "Hmmm, not bad, Mrs. Broussard."

"We'll have to remember this one for when we get good and desperate—maybe during hurricane season." agreed Helen.

Bea took a sip before continuing with something they had been discussing earlier. "So yes, dears, here's where my heart is calling. There is so much love and energy behind us and the Friendship Bench that Helen and I started realizing that it's a true ministry. Not your run-of-the-mill kind of ministry with a church and a steeple, but it certainly feels blessed. And I believe that the Lay Pastoral Assistance program I'm starting next week will only enhance what Helen and I started. Of course, I had already become an online minister, but that was just to perform the wedding. Now I'll be a Minister Plus!" she laughed. "That was so much fun looking at your faces when I started the ceremony!"

Helen spoke up, "I can't believe we both suddenly have to go to school for six months — me to the foster care classes and Bea to the Lay Ministry classes. I didn't see that coming!"

"So Bea," said Dawn, "If you're going through with this ministry thing, does that mean we have to call you Saint Bea?" She laughed out loud.

"It's a sin if you don't," said Bea with a straight face. All the sistahs laughed and yelled, "Saint Bea! I love it!"

"You really got everyone at that wedding, Saint Bea. It was just a complete shock and such a good surprise. And I couldn't agree with you more about the ministry program," said Helen, nodding. "I'm so proud of you for taking this next step. I'm a little envious in a way, but I figure you'll teach me all your new dance steps—so to speak—so we'll both learn something together. I'll be your Deaconess—or your Deacon John—whatever you want to call it. Meanwhile, I have my hands full."

"How is Cooper, by the way?" asked Judith. "Tell me quick because I have to take Lucy home before we go to hear Bitsy.

"He's settled into his room at home. And tomorrow, he and I are heading to New Orleans. Trinity is taking us out to lunch at

Antoine's with some movers and shakers she knows. She and Dawn are already determined that Cooper needs to go to LSU and then take the city by storm."

"Poor guy, nothing like being over-whelmed by those two," said Lola.

"Oh, that's nothing! Bea is even worse. Cooper doesn't stand a chance with all these crazy aunts. I'd pity him if I didn't think he actually loved it."

Bea looked over at her friend carefully and recognized the sheer, fierce happiness in Helen's face. She nodded, satisfied.

"Wait, "said Dawn. "I feel a bit slandered over here. I'm not an *overwhelming* auntie. I don't overwhelm! Remember, I didn't overwhelm your wedding."

"I didn't give you the chance," said Lola, laughing.

"Dawn, you're not still upset with us, are you?" asked Bud. "Please don't be. We had to pretend to be broken up because we wanted so much to have a calm, family-style, loving wedding. We knew that if we didn't pretend then we wouldn't be able to have that wedding. Everyone would have gone crazy with planning and we wouldn't have been able to stop them. You all know our families because you're part of them! They're unstoppable! We didn't mean to cause you all any trouble. I almost went crazy waiting for our wedding day, so we could tell everyone the big secret. If Lola and I hadn't snuck out together once in a while, I would be locked up in a very tight, wrap-around jacket by now. As it was, our wedding was so perfect — just what we wanted. The honeymoon wasn't too shabby either." He grinned at his wife.

Lola matched his smile. "Oh, stop. But seriously, I'm only gonna marry one man in this life because he's simply the right one. I'm just going to do it over and over again!"

The sistahs cracked up along with Bud, who said, "Oh Lord! I sure hope you're talking about me!"

Lola threw her arms around his broad shoulders, "Two weddings down, we'll just have to wait and see how many more there are to come."

"It could be our thing," said Bud. "We'll just keep getting married, but let's wait a few years till we do the next one, OK? I was so nervous for this one, you wouldn't believe it!"

Bea looked around smiling at her friends. "I have to say, there's so much love in this place. It's pure joy being here with y'all."

"Well, speaking of love," interrupted Dawn, "How is Marty, Judith? I'm so glad you two worked things out about Lillian. That could have been a real mess. And he's such a cutie!"

"It almost was a mess," said Judith, shaking her head, eyes wide. "I was afraid for a moment that it was all over. But when I explained what happened between Lillian and me, Marty just said that Lillian always had a flair for the dramatic. He had learned long ago not to get sucked in on her misadventures. Do I think we've heard the last from Lillian? No, not a chance. This is not over."

"What makes you say that, dear?" asked Bea.

Judith pulled a piece of paper out of her purse and held it up. "Because she sent me this email this morning."

She showed them. It simply read, "THIS IS NOT OVER."

"That woman!" said Lola.

Judith went on, "But Marty and I are fine right now." She laughed. "But I don't think I'll be going to his family gatherings anytime soon!"

"Oh boy," sighed Dawn. She got a mischievous look in her eyes and asked, "So…tell us, Judith. How is our romantic project going? Are there any love stars in those big, hazel eyes of yours yet?"

"Oh, Marty and I are taking it very slowly. In fact, if we were taking it any slower, we'd be walking backwards—which is just fine with me. But love? Hmmmmm…" She grabbed Lucy's pink leash, bent over, and picked up the wiggly, little pup in her arms. "I have to admit that I have fallen head over heels. And I think the feeling is mutual."

She nuzzled the puppy's head and was rewarded with a lick and a wagging, curled tail.

"Awww," said every one of them.

"Yep, things are final, as far as I'm concerned. No one has come to claim this little girl, and I've given them many chances. So Lucy and I are a family, and we're staying together."

"I don't blame you, Judith," said Bea. "She's a good catch."

"And that's good enough for now, ladies," said Judith and headed out the door. Just before it closed, she stuck her head back inside and quietly said, "One more thing—Marty told me that he was falling for me." Then the door closed behind her.

Dawn gasped and jumped straight out of her seat. "I knew it!" she crowed and ran after her. "Come back here, Judith Lafferty, we're not finished by a long shot!"

The End

GUMBEAUX SISTAHS RECIPES

GUMBEAUX SISTAHS
KITCHEN SINK COCKTAIL
CREATED BY ERIKA FREY

Makes 1 cocktail

1.5 OZ Whiskey
Big Splash Sparkling Apple Juice
1-2 T Lemon juice
Garnish with Black cherries in syrup
-Mix, pour over ice, and stir.

Cheers, Sistahs!

ROCKY'S GUMBO RICE

Great with gumbo or top with any *"Oh my gravy!"*

3 strips thick-cut bacon, cut up
1 cup long-grain white rice
1 yellow onion
1 tsp black pepper
1 tsp salt
1 tsp your favorite Cajun seasoning
2 cups chicken broth

Cook bacon in bottom of saucepan over medium heat. Remove from pan. Add onion and cook till almost tender. Stir in rice and cook, coating it with oil. When onion is tender and rice begins to brown lightly, put in salt, pepper, seasoning (if desired) and broth. Bring to a boil. Reduce heat to low, cover and simmer 20 minutes. Chop up cooked bacon and sprinkle on top when done. Serves 5 with gumbo.

DAWN'S POTATO SALAD
(FOR EATING WITH GUMBO
OR ALL BY ITSELF)

First, go to the market to shop—you know you will be out of something. Grab a bottle of wine while you are there too. All good cooks drink a little wine as they work!

INGREDIENTS:

5lb bag of red potatoes (white ones are too flaky)
5 eggs
Medium onion
Green onions—one bunch
1/4 pound of bacon, fried up and chopped
1 Jar—(30 fl oz) My-o-naise (mayonnaise!)—about 1/2 jar (more if you find it is too dry after mixing in)
½ c sweet Pickle relish
A splash of Zesty Italian Salad Dressing or red wine vinegar

GET COOKING:

1. Boil 8 to 10 (about 5 lbs) red potatoes.
2. Boil eggs

While they are boiling, chop one medium sized yellow onion very fine—to disguise it for those that say they don't like onions—and chop about one cup of green onions.

When the skin on the potatoes starts to crack, they are probably soft enough—not mushy. Pour them into a colander to cool a couple of minutes. I usually grab a pair of throw-away gloves and rub the skin off as soon as I can handle them. Let them sit and cool a little more before you cut them into bite-sized pieces, or they will crumble.

Peel and chop the eggs while you wait. Mash just one of the potatoes.

Put chopped potatoes and eggs in a large glass or plastic bowl. Don't mix them up yet.

Now get out that my-o-naise and add a tablespoon or two of salad dressing or wine vinegar, ¾ of the bacon pieces, chopped onion, pickle relish, salt, pepper, dash of garlic power and one mashed potato.

Fold it into the bowl as you mix the potatoes and eggs together.

Now top with green onions and the rest of the bacon pieces. (If you are using a deep bowl, put half of the potatoes/egg mixture in the bowl with the mayo and top with the green onions and bacon and then repeat with another layer of potato/egg mixture and topping. This way everyone gets some green onions and bacon topping!)

Enjoy with your favorite anything!

BITSY'S PRALINE CAKE
(WORTH THE TROUBLE!)

Cake
1 c butter
¼ c cocoa
1 c water
½ c buttermilk
2 lg eggs
1 tsp baking soda
1 tsp vanilla
2 c sugar
2 c all-purpose flour
½ tsp salt

Chocolate Ganache
1 c semi-sweet chocolate morsels
3 T heavy whipping cream
2 T butter, cut into pieces

Praline Frosting
¼ c butter
1 c firmly packed brown sugar
1/3 c whipping cream
1 c confectioners' sugar
1 tsp vanilla
1 c chopped pecans, toasted

DIRECTIONS

Cake:

- Preheat oven to 350 degrees and prepare cake pans
- Combine butter, cocoa and water in a saucepan.
- Cook, stirring constantly, over low heat until the mixture is smooth and butter has melted; remove from heat and cool.
- Combine the buttermilk, eggs, baking soda and vanilla; beat on medium speed with a mixer until smooth.
- Combine the butter mixture and buttermilk mixture; beat until well blended.
- Combine the sugar, flour and salt in a bowl; mix well.
- Gradually add the flour mixture to the buttermilk mixture; beat until blended.
- The batter should be thin.

- Spray three 8" round cake pans with cooking spray and line them with wax paper.
- Pour the batter evenly into the pans and bake at 350 degrees for 22-24 minutes or until cake tests for doneness.
- Cool in pans on wire racks for 10 minutes; remove from pans and cool completely.
- To assemble the cake:
- Spread 1/2 c ganache between the cake layers; spread the remainder on the sides of the cake and chill for 30 minutes.
- Slowly pour the frosting over the center of the cake.
- Spread it to the edges of the cake, allowing some frosting to run down the sides.

Chocolate Ganache:

- Microwave the chocolate and cream in a glass bowl for 2-3 minutes, or until the chocolate is melted; whisk until smooth
- Gradually add the butter, whisking until smooth and melted.
- Cool, whisking often, until spreading consistency, about 15-20 minutes.

Praline Frosting:

- Combine the butter, brown sugar and whipping cream in a 2 quart saucepan; bring to a boil, stirring often.
- Boil 1 min; remove from heat and whisk in powdered sugar and vanilla.
- Add the pecans and stir gently for 2-5 minutes, or until the frosting begins to cool and thicken slightly. Pour immediately over the cake

To assemble the cake:

- Spread 1/2 c ganache between the cake layers; spread the remainder on the sides of the cake and chill for 30 minutes.
- Slowly pour the frosting over the center of the cake.
- Spread it to the edges of the cake, allowing some frosting to run down the sides.

Then serve yourself a big piece before it's all gone!

ACKNOWLEDGEMENTS

First and foremost, I want to thank all the readers that wrote in asking for more stories about the Gumbeaux Sistahs. The Sistahs are not shy, you know, and they require very little encouragement to ham it up. It's so much fun making these women do and say the craziest things. And it's so satisfying having the Sistahs talk about the many challenges that face us in our lives. I hope I get to spend the rest of my life writing about the sistahs, their stories, their hearts, and their laughter. So to you, readers, I say a heartfelt "Thank you!"

To my editor, Elizabeth Frey, who lets me get away with absolutely nothing—dammit! To Staci Schwittay at James Samaritan for her help with questions about the foster care coordinating program. To Pastor Morgan MacIntire of Christ Episcopal Church for her suggestions on Pastoral Care Programs. To my sistahs: Ellen, Pemmie, Betty, Maurer, Sandra, Sue, Mary, Connie, and Cathy for all the wonderful Gumbeaux Sistahs photoshoots that were more about having a blast than about "getting the shot." To Dian Lusher for all her advice on everything in my life—from the book, to how I should clean my vegetables with vinegar! To my kids—Tony, Jessica, Erika, and Lizzy, for encouragement and affection when it was needed most.

To all the wonderful sistahs who showed up for the Gumbeaux Sistahs Second Line on Mardi Gras day, 2020, and making it SO MUCH FUN!

To my grandson, Catch. And to my granddaughter, Capri, who says I'm cool. Enough said right there.

With a great deal of love and gratitude,
Jax

ABOUT THE AUTHOR

Jax Frey

Born in New Orleans, Jax Frey came into this world with a sense of celebration of Louisiana culture, food, family, and fun. Translating that celebration into her writing and onto canvas is her true calling. Her colorful art depicts everything Louisiana, from her dancing Gumbeaux Sistahs paintings to her popular line of original Mini paintings. Because over 25,000 of the mini paintings have been created and sold into art collections worldwide, Jax holds a world record for *The Most Original Acrylic Paintings on Canvas by One Artist.*

    The Gumbeaux Sistahs is her debut novel, and *Gumbeaux Love* is the second book in the series. Jax is also the co-founder of the Women of Infinite Possibilities, an empowering women's organization started in Covington, LA, where Jax lives today with her loveable, tornado-of-a-pug named Lucy.

Contact Jax for her available dates for book
signings and speaking engagements.
Sign up for newsletter at: www.gumbeauxsistahs.com
FB and Instagram: Gumbeaux Sistahs
Jax's art can be seen at: www.artbyjax.com
FB and Instagram: Jax Frey

WE LOVE REVIEWS!

Dear Readers:

Please share your reading experience of The Gumbeaux **Sistahs** novels:

- o   Help others make good book choices
- o   Help your authors get the word out about their work.

Simply leave a review of *The Gumbeaux Sistahs* or *Gumbeaux Love* on Amazon.

Here's how to leave a review:

- -   Just go to www.Amazon.com and search for either *The Gumbeaux Sistahs* or *Gumbeaux Love (or both!)*
- -   Click on the book title.
- -   Scroll down to find the *Review This Product* section to leave your review.

Here are some recent reviews to give you an example—the review can be long or short, it doesn't matter—they are all appreciated and helpful!

"I LOVED THIS BOOK. I CAN SO RELATE TO THIS BOOK. PEOPLE IN LOUISIANA ARE

LIKE THIS! I can't wait to share this book with my sister's!"

"I absolutely LOVED this book, the style and description of characters. I went on a cruise and read this book in 1 day! I couldn't put it down. GREAT book especially if you know the area it takes place in. It's about community, helping one another out and just doing life together. A MUST read in your collection! Oprah needs to endorse it!! Just saying!"

"This is a great read for immersing yourself in the fun loving, warmhearted, feel good camaraderie that abounds in small Southern towns. The characters are quirky and interesting, and find solutions to life's challenges over great gumbo and great wine. Just like my friends and me!"

And please copy and paste your Amazon review into your Facebook and Instagram accounts—thanks so very much for the Gumbeaux Sistah love!

OTHER BOOKS BY JAX FREY

The Gumbeaux Sistahs
(The First book in Gumbeaux Sistahs series)

Five, fiery, Southern women wage a hilarious war against the problems of a sistah-in-trouble using their improbable friendships, unpredictable schemes, oh-so-numerous cocktails, and a shared passion for good gumbo. The Gumbeaux Sistahs is a heart-warming, laugh-out-loud story you won't want to put down.

An official selection of the Pulpwood Queens—the largest book club in the world with over 800 book clubs registered.
Available at Amazon.com and
Signed paperback copics at www.gumbcauxsistahs.com

Coming Soon!

More adventures with the Gumbeaux Sistahs novels!

Join the Gumbeaux Sistahs online and be one of the first to know when the next book in the Gumbeaux Sistahs series is out!

www.gumbeauxsistahs.com

Free Gift

Sign up for Gumbeaux Sistahs newsletter
to receive **Free Gifts** including:

1. The latest and greatest of The Gumbeaux Sistah's Best
    Recipes ever!
    and
2. A free pdf version of:
    18 Gumbeaux Sistahs Steps to Living Happily Ever After

These are 18 Life Lesson Steps that can change your life forever.
Try them today!

Get your free gifts with signup at www.gumbeauxsistahs.com

READERS' GUIDE
GUMBEAUX LOVE
BY JAX FREY

1.   *What three words would you use to best describe this book?*

2.   *What was your favorite moment in the book? Your least favorite?*

3.   *If you were in charge of casting the movie version of this book, who would you cast as each character?*

4.   *If you could invite one character over to your house for dinner, who would it be & why?*

5. *If you had to trade places with any character in the book, who would you choose & why?*

6. *What surprised you the most when you were reading this book?*

7. *How did the setting of the book impact the story?*

8. *If you had to choose one lesson that the author was trying to teach us with this story, what would it be?*

9. *If you could write one more chapter after the ending, what would you write?*

Lucy

Made in the USA
Columbia, SC
24 November 2024

47437632R00152